PRESENTED TO

GILLIAN GRANT

for

Sunday School Attendance

1976/77

PICKERING & INGLIS LTD.   PRINTED IN GREAT BRITAIN

THE ADVENTURES OF PINOCCHIO

THE ADVENTURES OF PINOCCHIO

by

CARLO COLLODI

THE CHILDREN'S PRESS

LONDON AND GLASGOW

This Impression 1976

ISBN 0 00 166006 3

PRINTED AND MADE IN GREAT BRITAIN

CONTENTS

CHAPTER ONE

*How it Happened that Mr. Cherry, the Carpenter, Found a
Piece of Wood that Laughed and Cried Like a Baby*

ONCE upon a time there was . . .

" A king ! " my small readers will exclaim. No, children,
you are mistaken. Once upon a time there was a piece of
wood.

It was not the best wood, but just a common piece, such as
we use in stoves and fireplaces to kindle a fire and warm our
rooms in winter.

I can't say how it happened, but the fact is that one fine day
this piece of wood happened to be in the shop of an old carpenter
whose name was Mr. Antonio, but everyone called him Mr.
Cherry, because the end of his nose was always red and shiny
like a ripe cherry.

As soon as Mr. Cherry saw this piece of wood, he was very
pleased : he rubbed his hands together joyfully, and said to
himself :

" This has come in the nick of time ; it is just what I want
to make a leg for my little table."

Without losing a moment he took his sharp hatchet, and was
going to strip off the bark and trim it into shape. But just as he
raised the hatchet to strike the first blow, he paused with his
hand in the air, for he heard a tiny, tiny voice which said
warningly :

" Don't strike me too hard ! "

Imagine Mr. Cherry's surprise !

He glanced around the shop in a fright to see where that little
voice could have come from, but he saw no one. He looked
under his bench. No one. He looked in a cupboard which
he always kept locked ; but there was no one. He looked in
his basket of chips and sawdust. No one. He opened the

shop door and looked out into the street, and no one! What then?

"I see," he said at last, laughing and scratching his wig, "I must have imagined that little voice. Let us get to work."

He took up his hatchet again, and down it came on the piece of wood.

"Oh, you hurt me!" whimpered that same little voice.

This time Mr. Cherry was thunderstruck. His eyes stood out of his head with fear; his mouth was wide open, and his tongue hung down over his chin like a mask at a fountain.

As soon as he could speak he said, trembling and stammering in fright:

"But where did that little voice come from that cried 'Oh'? There's not a living soul here. Can it be that this piece of wood has learned to cry and complain like a baby? I can't believe it. This piece of wood—look at it! It's just a piece of firewood, like all the others; when you put it on the fire it will help to boil a kettle. Well, then? Is someone hidden inside it? If there is, so much the worse for him. I'll attend to his case!"

With these words he grasped that poor piece of wood with both hands, and began to beat it against the wall without mercy.

Then he stopped and listened to see if any little voice was complaining this time. He waited two minutes—nothing: five minutes—nothing; ten minutes—and still nothing!

"Now I understand," he exclaimed, laughing and rumpling his wig. "I must have imagined that little voice that said 'Oh!' Let us get to work."

And because he felt very much afraid, he began to sing to give himself courage.

Meanwhile he put the hatchet down and taking up his plane he began to plane and shape the piece of wood. But while the plane went back and forth, he heard again that little voice which said, laughing:

"Stop! you're tickling me!"

This time poor Mr. Cherry dropped as if struck by lightning. When he opened his eyes he was sitting on the floor.

He was so changed you would hardly have recognised him. Even the end of his nose, which was always crimson, had turned blue with fright.

Chapter Two

*Mr. Cherry Gives the Piece of Wood to his Friend Geppetto,
who Plans a Marvellous Marionette that can Dance, and
Fence, and Turn Somersaults in the Air*

At that moment someone rapped on the door.

" Come in," said the carpenter, but he did not have strength
enough to get up.

A little, lively old man walked into the shop. His name was
Geppetto, but when the boys in the neighbourhood wanted to
tease him, they called him by his nickname of Polendina, on
account of his yellow wig which looked very much like a dish
of *polenta*, which is like porridge.

Geppetto was very quick-tempered. Woe to him who called
him Polendina! He simply went wild, and no one could do
anything with him.

" Good morning, Mr. Antonio," said Geppetto, "what are
you doing down there ? "

" I am teaching the ants their letters."

" Much good may it do you ! "

" What brought you here, Mr. Geppetto ? "

" My legs. Do you know, Mr. Antonio, I have come to ask
a favour of you."

" Here I am, ready to serve you," replied the carpenter,
getting to his knees.

" I had an idea this morning."

" Let us hear it."

" I thought I would make a fine wooden marionette, a really
wonderful one, that could dance, and fence, and turn somersaults in the air. Then, with this marionette, I would travel
round the world, and earn my bit of bread and my glass of wine.
What do you think of that ? "

" Bravo, Polendina ! " cried that same little, mysterious
voice.

When he heard himself called Polendina, Mr. Geppetto
became so angry that he turned as red as a ripe pepper-pod.
He whirled on the carpenter, and said in a rage:

" Why do you offend me ? "

" Who is offending you ? "

" You called me Polendina ! "

" No, indeed I didn't ! "

" Oh ! perhaps *I* said it ! But I say that it was you."

" No ! "

" Yes ! "

" No ! "

" Yes ! "

And getting more and more excited, from words they came
to blows. They snatched at one another's wigs, and even slapped
and bit and scratched each other.

At the end of the combat Mr. Antonio found Geppetto's
yellow wig in his hands, and Geppetto had the carpenter's grey
wig between his teeth.

" Give me my wig," said Mr. Antonio.

" And you give me mine, and let us make a treaty of peace."

So the two little old men, after each had put on his own wig,
shook hands, and vowed to be good friends as long as they both
should live.

" Now, neighbour Geppetto," said the carpenter, to show
that they were friends again, " what is it that I can do for you ? "

" I would like a little piece of wood to make my marionette."

Mr. Antonio, well pleased, went quickly to his bench, and
took the piece of wood which had given him such a fright. But
just as he was giving it to his friend it shook so hard that it
slipped out of his hands, and struck poor Geppetto violently on
the shin.

" Ah ! this is a fine way to make me a present, Mr. Antonio !
You have almost lamed me."

" Upon my honour, I didn't do it ! "

" Oh ! so *I* did it then ! "

" It's all the fault of this piece of wood . . ."

" Yes, I know the wood struck me, but you threw it at my legs ! "

" I did not throw it at you ! "

" That's a falsehood ! "

" Geppetto, don't insult me ; if you do I will call you Polendina ! "

" Blockhead ! "

" Polendina ! "

" Donkey ! "

" Polendina ! "

" Ugly monkey ! "

" Polendina ! "

When he heard himself called Polendina for the third time, Geppetto, blind with rage, rushed at the carpenter, and the second battle was worse than the first.

When it was over, Mr. Antonio had two more scratches on his nose, and the other two buttons less on his jacket. The accounts thus being even, they shook hands again, and vowed to be good friends as long as they both should live. Then Geppetto took his piece of wood, and after thanking Mr. Antonio, went limping home.

CHAPTER THREE

Geppetto Goes Home and Makes his Marionette : he Calls Him
Pinocchio : the Marionette Gets into Mischief

GEPPETTO lived in a little room on the ground floor that was
lighted by a window under the stairs. His furniture could not
have been simpler. A rickety chair, a shaky bed, and a broken-
down table. At the back of the room a fireplace could be seen,
with the fire lighted ; but the fire was painted, and over the fire
was a painted kettle which was boiling merrily, and sending
forth a cloud of steam that was just like real steam.

As soon as he came home, Geppetto took his tools and began
to carve his marionette.

"What shall I call him ? " he said to himself. "I think
I will call him Pinocchio. This name will bring him good luck.
I once knew a whole family of Pinocchios : there was Pinocchio
the father, and Pinocchia the mother, and Pinocchii the children,
and they all got along splendidly. The richest of them was a
beggar."

When he had thought of a name for his marionette, he set
to work with a will. He made his hair, and his forehead, and
his eyes in a very short time.

As soon as the eyes were finished, imagine his amazement
when he saw them move, and look at him intently.

When Geppetto saw those two wooden eyes watching him,
he didn't like it at all, and he said crossly :

"Naughty wooden eyes, why are you looking at me ? "

But no one answered.

After the eyes he made the nose ; but as soon as it was
finished, it began to grow. It grew, and it grew, until in a few
minutes it was so long that it seemed as if there was no end to it.

Poor Geppetto worked fast to shorten it, but the more he
pared it down and cut it off, the longer that impertinent nose
became.

After the nose he made the mouth ; but before he had finished with it, it began to laugh and make fun of him.

" Stop laughing ! " said Geppetto irritably, but he might as well have spoken to the wall.

" Stop laughing, I say ! " he shouted in a menacing voice.

The mouth stopped laughing, and stuck out its tongue.

However since Geppetto did not want to spoil the marionette, he pretended not to see it, and went on with his work.

After the mouth he made the chin, then the neck, the shoulders, the stomach, the arms, and the hands.

The moment the hands were finished, Geppetto's wig was snatched from his head. He glanced upwards, and what did he see ? There was his yellow wig in the marionette's hands.

" Pinocchio ! Give me back my wig this moment ! "

But Pinocchio, instead of returning the wig, put it on his own head, and was almost hidden under it.

This insolent, mocking behaviour made Geppetto feel sadder than ever before in all his life. He turned to Pinocchio and said :

" You rogue of a son ! You are not yet finished, and you begin to disobey your father ! That's bad, my boy, very bad ! "

And he wiped away a tear.

There were still the legs and feet to make.

When Geppetto had finished the feet, a kick landed on his nose.

" It serves me right," he said to himself. " I should have thought of that before ! Now it is too late."

He took the marionette in his hands and placed him on the floor to see if he could walk ; but Pinocchio's legs were stiff, and he didn't know how to move them. So Geppetto took him by the hand, and showed him how to put one foot before the other.

When the stiffness was out of his legs, Pinocchio began to walk alone, and run around the room ; and finally he slipped out of the door into the street and ran away.

Poor old Geppetto ran after him as fast as he could, but he could not catch him, for the little scamp jumped like a rabbit, and his wooden feet clattered on the pavement, making as much noise as twenty pairs of wooden shoes.

" Catch him ! Catch him ! " cried Geppetto; but when the people saw that wooden marionette running as fast as a racehorse, they stared at him in amazement, and then laughed, and laughed, and laughed, until their sides were sore.

At last, by some lucky chance, a policeman appeared. When he heard such a clatter he thought somebody's horse had got away from its master ; so he courageously planted himself in the middle of the street with his legs wide apart, determined to stop it and prevent any further trouble.

While Pinocchio was still a long way off he saw the policeman barricading the street, and he decided to run between his legs before he realised what he meant to do ; but he failed dismally.

The policeman, without moving from his position, picked him up neatly by the nose (that ridiculous, long nose, that seemed made on purpose to be seized by policemen) and returned him to Geppetto, who meant to pull his ears well to punish him for his naughtiness. Imagine, therefore, how he felt when he couldn't find any ears : and do you know why ? Because he had made him in such a hurry that he had forgotten his ears.

So he took him by the nape of his neck, and as they walked away he said, shaking his head threateningly :

" Come along home. I will settle accounts with you when we get there ! "

At this ominous remark Pinocchio threw himself down on the ground and refused to walk any farther. A crowd of idlers and inquisitive people gathered around him.

Some said one thing, some another.

" The poor marionette ! " some of them exclaimed, " he is right in not wanting to go home ! Who knows how dreadfully that bad Geppetto might beat him ! "

And others added maliciously :

" Geppetto *seems* like a good man, but he is a perfect tyrant with children. If we leave that poor marionette in his hands, he is capable of tearing him to pieces ! "

In short, so much was said and done that the policeman let
Pinocchio go, and decided to take poor Geppetto to prison. He
was not able for the moment to say anything in his own defence,
but cried like a calf, and as they walked towards the prison he
sobbed :

" Wretched son ! And to think that I worked so hard to make
a fine marionette ! But I deserve it. I ought to have known
what would happen ! "

What happened afterwards is almost too much to believe ;
and I will tell you about it in the following chapters.

CHAPTER FOUR

*The Story of Pinocchio and the Talking Cricket in which it is
Shown that Children do not Like to be Corrected by those who
are Wiser than they are*

NOW I must tell you, children, that while poor Geppetto was
taken to prison for no fault of his own, that scamp Pinocchio,
left to himself, ran away across the fields in order to get home
as quickly as possible. In his haste he jumped over high banks,
thorn hedges, and ditches full of water, like a little goat, or a
hare running from the hunters.

When he got home, he found the door ajar. Pushing it open,
he went in, and locked it securely after him. Then he threw
himself down on the floor with a great sigh of relief.

But the relief did not last long, for he heard something in
the room saying:

" Cri-cri-cri ! "

" Who is calling me ? " said Pinocchio in a fright.

" It is I."

Pinocchio turned and saw a large cricket crawling slowly up
the wall.

" Speak to me, Cricket. Who are you ? "

" I am the Talking Cricket, and I have lived in this room
for more than a hundred years."

" But to-day this is my room, and you will oblige me by going
away immediately, without even looking behind you."

" I shall not leave this place," replied the Cricket, " until I
have told you a very unpleasant truth."

" Well, then, tell me, and be quick about it ! "

" Woe to those children who rebel against their parents, and
who run away from their homes. They will never be happy in
this world, and sooner or later they will repent it bitterly."

" Sing away, Cricket, just as you please ; but to-morrow, at sunrise, I am going to leave; for if I stay here it will happen to me just as it happens to other children: I shall be sent to school and, by love or by force, I shall be made to study. Now I will tell you in confidence that I don't intend to study at all; I should be far happier chasing butterflies, and climbing trees to rob birds' nests."

" You poor simpleton! Don't you know that, if you spend your time in that way, you will grow up to be a great donkey, and everyone will laugh at you? "

" Be still, you croaking Cricket! " cried Pinocchio.

But the Cricket, who was patient, and also a philosopher, instead of being offended by such impertinence, proceeded in the same tone as before:

" And if you don't like to go to school, why don't you learn a trade? Then you could, at least, earn your bread honestly."

" Do you want me to tell you something? " retorted Pinocchio, who was beginning to lose his patience. " Among all the trades in the world there is only one which really suits me."

" And what might that be? "

" To eat, drink, sleep, and amuse myself, and to lead a vagabond life from morning to night."

" Let me say for your information," said the Talking Cricket, calm and patient as usual, " that those who follow that trade finish, almost always, in a hospital or a prison."

" Be careful, you Cricket of bad omen! If you make me angry, the worse for you! "

" Poor Pinocchio! I am really sorry for you! "

" Why are you sorry for me? "

" Because you are a marionette, and what is worst of all you have a wooden head."

At these last words Pinocchio lost his temper entirely. He seized a mallet from the bench, and threw it at the Cricket.

Perhaps he did not intend to hit him but unluckily the mallet struck him right on the head. The poor Cricket had only time to cry " Cri-cri-cri," and there he was stretched out stiff, but still clinging to the wall.

CHAPTER FIVE

Pinocchio is Hungry, and he Looks for an Egg to Make an Omelette : but just as he Breaks it in the Pan the Omelette flies out of the Window

IT began to grow dark, and Pinocchio remembered that he had had nothing to eat. There was an uncomfortable feeling in his stomach that closely resembled appetite.

With children appetite grows fast. In fact, after a few minutes it became hunger, and in no time at all he was as hungry as a wolf, so hungry he could have eaten nails.

Poor Pinocchio ran to the fireplace where the kettle was boiling and put out his hand to lift the cover and see what was in it but the kettle was painted on the wall. What a disappointment ! His nose, which was already too long, grew several inches longer.

He ran about the room and searched in every dish and cupboard for a little bread—even dry bread—yes, he would have been thankful for a crust, or a bone left by a dog, or a fishbone or cherry stone, in short, anything he could chew on ; but he found nothing, just nothing, absolutely nothing.

Meanwhile he grew hungrier every moment, and there was nothing left to do but yawn. He yawned such enormous yawns that his mouth reached away back to his ears ; and after he yawned, he spat, and it seemed as if he hadn't any stomach left.

At last, in despair, he began to weep, saying :

" The Talking Cricket was right. I did wrong to rebel against my father and run away. If my father were here now, I shouldn't be yawning myself to death. Oh, hunger is a dreadful disease ! "

Suddenly in a pile of rubbish he saw something white and round that looked like an egg. Instantly he pounced upon it. It really was an egg.

It would be impossible to describe his joy; you must imagine it. He feared he might be dreaming. He rolled the egg from one hand to the other, he patted it and kissed it as he said :

" Now how shall I cook it ? Shall I make an omelette ? No, it would be better to poach it. But perhaps it would be more tasty if I fried it ; or shall I cook it in the shell ? No, the quickest way would be to poach it. I cannot wait to eat it."

No sooner said than done. He set a little stewpan over a brazier of lighted charcoal, put some water in it, instead of oil or butter, and when the water began to boil, tac ! he broke the eggshell and held it over the pan.

But instead of the yolk and white of an egg, a little chicken flew out gaily, and making a polite bow, said cheerfully :

" A thousand thanks, Mr. Pinocchio, for having spared me the trouble of breaking the shell ! Good-bye, take care of yourself, and give my love to the folks ! "

With that the chicken spread its wings and, flying through the open window, was soon lost to sight.

The poor marionette stood there as if hypnotised, with his eyes fixed in his head, his mouth open, and the pieces of eggshell in his hands. When he recovered a little from his first fright, he began to cry, and scream, and stamp on the floor in despair ; and as he wept he said :

" Yes, the Talking Cricket was right ! If I hadn't run away from home, and if my father were only here, I should not now be dying of hunger. Oh, hunger is a dreadful disease ! "

His stomach felt emptier than ever, and since he could find nothing to put into it he thought he would go out again into the village, in the hope of meeting some charitable person who would give him a little bread.

CHAPTER SIX

Pinocchio Goes to Sleep with his Feet on the Brazier, and when he Wakes up in the Morning they are Burned off

IT was a bitterly cold night. The thunder rolled, and the lightning flashed as though the heavens were afire. A fierce wind whistled angrily, raising clouds of dust, and making all the trees writhe and groan as if in torment.

Pinocchio was dreadfully afraid of thunder and lightning, but his hunger was greater than his fear, so he opened the door and hurried as fast as he could to the village, arriving there with his tongue hanging out like a hunting dog's.

But all was dark and silent. The shops were closed, the doors of the houses were closed, the windows were closed, and there was not even a dog to be seen in the street. It seemed a village of the dead.

However, Pinocchio, conquered by hunger and despair, gave a long, long ring at the door of one of the houses, saying to himself:

" Someone will certainly look out ! "

And in fact a lively old man with a nightcap on his head looked out of a window and shouted crossly :

" What do you want at this hour ? "

" Will you be so good as to give me a piece of bread ? "

" Wait ! I'll be right back ! " replied the old man, believing that he had to do with one of those scapegraces who amuse themselves at night by ringing doorbells, and annoying good people who want to sleep in peace.

In half a minute the window was opened again, and the same voice called to Pinocchio :

" Stand under the window, and hold up your cap ! "

Pinocchio had never yet had a cap, but he stood under the window, and a great kettleful of water rained down on him, drenching him from head to foot, as if he had been a wilted geranium.

He went home wet as a drowned rat, and almost dead with fatigue and hunger. He could not stand up any longer, and so he sat down, and put his wet, muddy feet on the warm brazier.

In this position he fell asleep, and while he was asleep his feet, which were of wood, caught fire and slowly burned away to ashes.

Pinocchio slept and snored as if his feet belonged to someone else. At last, at daybreak, he was roused by someone rapping on the door.

" Who is it ? " he called, yawning and rubbing his eyes.

" It is I ! " replied a voice.

That voice was the voice of Geppetto.

CHAPTER SEVEN

*Geppetto Comes Home, and Gives the Marionette the Break-
fast that the Poor Man had Brought for himself*

POOR Pinocchio's eyes were still half-shut, and he had not
noticed that his feet were burned away; so when he heard his
father's voice he jumped down from his stool to run and draw
the bolt, but after staggering a little he fell his full length on the
floor, making a noise as if a whole bag of wooden spoons had
fallen from the fifth storey.

" Open the door ! " cried Geppetto.

" I can't, Daddy," replied the marionette, bursting into tears
and rolling over and over on the floor.

" Why not ? "

" Because someone has eaten my feet ! "

" And who has eaten them ? "

" The cat," said Pinocchio, seeing the cat who was just then
playing with some shavings.

" Open the door, I tell you ! " cried Geppetto again; " if
you don't I'll give you the cat-o'-nine-tails when I get in ! "

" Truly, I can't stand up. Oh, poor me ! poor me ! I shall
have to walk on my knees all the rest of my life ! "

Geppetto, thinking that all this lamenting was just another
of the marionette's tricks, decided to end it once and for all.
He climbed up on the wall, and went in at the window.

At first he was furious ; but when he saw his own Pinocchio
lying on the floor, and actually without any feet, his anger
melted away. He took him up in his arms, kissed and caressed
him, and with tears running down his cheeks, he said, as well
as he could for sobbing :

" My dear little Pinocchio, how did your feet get burned
away ? "

" I don't know, Daddy, but believe me it has been a dreadful night. I shall never forget it as long as I live. It thundered

and lightened, and I was so hungry, and the Talking Cricket said : ' It serves you right ; you have been naughty and you deserve it ! ' and I said : ' Be careful, Cricket ! ' and he said : ' You are a marionette with a wooden head ! ' and I threw the mallet at him, and he died, but it was his fault, for I didn't want to kill him, and the proof of that is that I put the stewpan on the brazier, but the chicken flew away and said : ' Good-bye, give my love to the folks ! ' and I got hungrier every moment, and that's the reason that little old man with the nightcap on puts his head out of the window, and said : ' Stand under the window and hold up your cap,' and there I was with a whole kettleful of water on my head, and it isn't a disgrace to ask for a bit of bread, is it ? I ran back home as fast as I could, and because I was so dreadfully hungry I put my feet on the brazier to dry them, and then you came home, and my feet were burned off, and I'm still so hungry, and I haven't any feet ! Boo-hoo-hoo ! "

And poor Pinocchio began to cry and scream so loudly that he could have been heard for miles around.

Geppetto had only understood one thing in all this jumble of words ; and that was that the marionette was dying of hunger. He took three pears out of his pocket, and said as he gave them to him :

" These three pears were for my breakfast ; but I gladly give them to you. Eat them, and may they do you good."

" If you want me to eat them, you must pare them for me."

" Pare them for you ? " cried Geppetto in astonishment. " I would never have believed, my son, that you were so finicky and full of odd notions. That's too bad ! We should accustom ourselves from childhood to eat whatever is set before us, and be thankful to get it ; because one never knows what might happen. This is a curious world."

" That's all very well," retorted Pinocchio, " but I shall never eat any fruit that isn't pared. I can't abide parings."

So that patient, kind Geppetto took out his pocket-knife and pared the three pears, putting all the parings on the corner of the table.

When Pinocchio had made two mouthfuls of the first pear, he was about to throw away the core, but Geppetto stopped him.

" Don't throw it away, there might be some use for it."

" Do you imagine I would eat the core ? " cried Pinocchio, turning on him in a rage.

" Who knows ! This is a curious world," replied Geppetto calmly.

So the three cores, instead of being thrown out of the window were put on the corner of the table to keep the parings company.

When he had eaten or rather devoured the three pears, Pinocchio stretched himself, yawned, and then began to whine:

" I'm hungry again ! "

" But, my son, I have nothing more to give you."

" Nothing, nothing at all ? "

" These parings and cores are all I have."

" Patience ! " said Pinocchio, " if there's really nothing else, I might eat a bit of paring."

And he began forthwith. At first he grimaced over it, but one after another all the parings quickly disappeared ; and after them the cores ; and when he had eaten everything, he patted his stomach and said cheerfully :

" Now I feel better ! "

" You see," said Geppetto, " that I was right when I said you should not be so dainty and particular about your food. My dear boy, one never knows what may happen. This is a curious world."

CHAPTER EIGHT

Geppetto Makes Pinocchio Some New Feet, and Sells his Own Coat to Buy him a Primer

JUST as soon as the marionette had satisfied his hunger, he began to whimper and grumble because he wanted some new feet.

But Geppetto, in order to punish him for all his naughtiness, let him cry and complain a whole half-day. At last he said :

" Why should I make you new feet ? So that you can run away from home again ? "

" I promise," said the sobbing marionette, " that from this day forth I will be good."

" That's just what all children say when they want something," replied Geppetto.

" I promise to go to school, and study, and make you proud of me . . ."

" All children say that very thing when they want something."

" But I'm not like other children ! I am better than any of them, and I always tell the truth. I promise you, Daddy, that I will learn a trade, and become the staff and consolation of your old age."

Although Geppetto tried to look very fierce, his eyes were full of tears, and his heart was very sad when he saw his poor Pinocchio in that dreadful state. He did not say another word, but he took up his tools and two little pieces of seasoned wood and began to work as hard as he could.

In less than half an hour the feet were done ; two slender, nimble, swift little feet that might have been carved by a real artist.

Then Geppetto said :

" Shut your eyes and go to sleep. I want to surprise you."

Pinocchio shut his eyes, and pretended to go to sleep ; and while he was pretending Geppetto melted some glue in an eggshell, and fastened the feet in place ; and he did it so neatly that you could not even see where they were joined to his legs.

As soon as the marionette felt that he had feet again, he jumped down from the table where he was lying and began to caper and dance around, fairly crazy with joy.

" Now to show you how grateful I am," said Pinocchio to his father, " I want to go right to school."

" What a good boy ! "

" But if I'm going to school I need some clothes."

Geppetto was a poor man : he hadn't a penny in his pocket : so he made Pinocchio a suit out of flowered paper, a pair of shoes out of bark, and a cap out of a soft piece of bread.

Pinocchio ran to look at himself in a basin full of water, and he was so pleased that he said as he strutted about :

" I look just like a gentleman ! "

" Yes, indeed," replied Geppetto, " but remember, it is not fine clothes that make a gentleman, but rather, clean clothes."

" Speaking of school," continued Pinocchio, " there's still something lacking, and it's the most important and necessary of all."

" And that is . . ? "

" I have no primer."

" That's right ; but how shall we get one ? "

" That is easy ! Go to the bookshop and buy one."

" And the money ? "

" I haven't any."

" Neither have I," added the good old man sadly.

Pinocchio became sad, too, although he was usually very cheerful ; for poverty, when it is real poverty, destroys all joy, even in children.

" Patience ! " cried Geppetto suddenly, and jumping up he put on his old fustian coat, all holes and patches, and ran out of the house.

B.

In a little while he was back again with a primer in his hand for his son ; but the poor man was in his shirt-sleeves, and it was snowing outside.

" Where is your coat, Daddy ? "

" I have sold it."

" Why did you sell it ? "

" It made me too warm."

Pinocchio understood instantly, and he was so overcome that he threw his arms around Geppetto's neck and kissed him all over his face.

CHAPTER NINE

Pinocchio Sells his Primer in Order to See the Marionettes

WHEN it stopped snowing, Pinocchio took his fine new primer under his arm, and started for school. On the way he made all sorts of fine plans, and built a thousand air castles, each one more beautiful than the other.

He began saying to himself :

" At school to-day I will learn to read immediately ; to-morrow I will learn to write, and day after to-morrow I will learn arithmetic. Then I shall be so well educated that I can earn heaps of money ; and with the very first pennies I earn I will buy my father a nice new cloth coat. But why do I say cloth ? It shall be all of gold and silver, with diamond buttons. That poor man really deserves it, for in order that I may get an education he stripped off his coat to buy me a book—in this cold weather ! Only a father would make such a sacrifice ! "

While he was saying this, and becoming more and more excited, he heard the music of fife and drum in the distance : fi-fi-fi . . . zum, zum, zum, zum.

He stopped and listened. The sounds came from the end of a long street that crossed the one which led to school. At the end of it there was a little village close to the sea.

" What can that music be ? What a shame that I have to go to school ! If it weren't for that . . ."

He hesitated. At any rate, he must decide either to go to school or to listen to the fifes.

" To-day I will listen to the fifes, and to-morrow I will go to school. There's always time to go to school," said that bad boy, shrugging his shoulders.

No sooner said than done. He ran down the cross-street as fast as he could go. The farther he ran the more distinctly he heard the tune the fifes were playing, and the beating of the big drum : fi-fi-fi, fi-fi-fi, fi-fi-fi . . . zum, zum, zum, zum.

All at once he found himself in a little square full of people who were crowding around a great, gaily-painted building of boards and cloth.

" What is that big building ? " inquired Pinocchio, turning to a boy who seemed to live there.

" Read the poster if you want to know."

" I would gladly read it, but I don't know how to read to-day."

" Bravo, simpleton ! Then I'll read it for you. Know then that in that big poster with the letters red as fire it is written :

" GREAT MARIONETTE THEATRE "

" Is it long since the play began ? "

" It's just beginning."

" How much does it cost to go in ? "

" Twopence."

Pinocchio was so consumed with curiosity that he lost his wits, and without any shame he said to the boy :

" Will you give me twopence until to-morrow ? "

" I would just love to," said the boy, laughing at him, " but I can't do it to-day."

" I will sell you my jacket for twopence," said the marionette.

" What would I do with a jacket of flowered paper ? If it should rain, I couldn't take it off."

" Will you buy my shoes ? "

" They're only good for firewood."

" What will you give me for my cap ? "

" That would be a fine bargain ! A cap made of bread ! The rats might eat it right off my head ! "

Pinocchio was on pins and needles. He was almost ready to make one more offer, but he lacked the courage. He hesitated, and stammered, and at last he said :

" Will you give me twopence for this new primer ? "

" I am only a boy, and I do not buy things from other boys," said the other, who had much more sense than Pinocchio.

" I'll give you twopence for the primer," cried an old-clothes man who had overheard the conversation.

The book was sold instantly. And only to think that poor Geppetto was at home shivering in his shirt-sleeves, because he had sold his coat to buy that primer for his son !

CHAPTER TEN

*The Marionettes Recognise Pinocchio as One of their Family
and are Delighted to See him, but Fire-Eater, the Showman,
Appears in the Midst of their Joy, and Pinocchio almost
Comes to a Dreadful End*

WHEN Pinocchio entered the marionette theatre he nearly
caused a riot.

You see, the curtain was up and the play had begun.

Harlequin and Punchinello were on the stage and quarrelling
as usual, threatening every moment to come to blows.

The audience were paying the closest attention. They laughed
until their sides were sore to see those two marionettes
quarrel, and gesticulate, and call each other names. It was just
as if they were really two reasoning animals, two real human
beings.

But all at once Harlequin stopped playing his part, and,
turning towards the public and pointing to the back of the
theatre, he shouted in his best dramatic manner:

" Heavens above! Am I awake, or am I dreaming? That
is certainly Pinocchio back there ! "

" Yes, it's really Pinocchio ! " cried Punchinello.

" 'Tis he, indeed ! " exclaimed Signora Rosaura, putting her
head out at the back of the stage.

" Here's Pinocchio ! Here's Pinocchio ! " shouted all the
marionettes in chorus, running out of the wings. " Here's
Pinocchio ! Here's our brother Pinocchio ! Hurray for
Pinocchio ! "

" Come up here to me, Pinocchio," cried Harlequin,
" come and throw yourself into the arms of your wooden
brother ! "

At this affectionate invitation Pinocchio made one jump from
the back of the theatre to the front seats ; another jump, and

he landed on the head of the orchestra leader, and from there he made a flying leap to the stage.

It is impossible to describe the hubbub which followed : the hugging and kissing, the friendly pinches, the brotherly thumps which Pinocchio received from the actors and actresses of that puppet company.

I can only say that it was a thrilling spectacle. But the audience, when they saw that the play was not going forward, became impatient and began to shout :

" The play ! The play ! Go on with the play ! "

However, their breath was wasted, for the marionettes, instead of getting on with it, redoubled their tumultuous cries of joy and, placing Pinocchio on their shoulders, they carried him in triumph down to the footlights.

Suddenly the puppet Showman appeared. He was very tall, and so ugly that it frightened one only to look at him. His beard was like a smear of black ink, and it was so long that it came down to the ground, so that he stepped on it when he walked. His mouth was as large as an oven ; his eyes were like two red lanterns, and he was cracking a great whip made of serpents' and foxes' tails, twisted together.

When the Showman appeared so unexpectedly no one breathed. You could have heard a pin drop. All those poor marionettes trembled like so many leaves.

" Why have you come here to disturb my theatre ? " he asked Pinocchio, in a voice like that of an ogre with a bad cold.

" Believe me, Your Honour, it was not my fault."

" Not another word ! We will settle our accounts to-night."

As soon as the play was over, the Showman went into the kitchen, where a whole sheep which he was roasting for his supper was slowly turning on the spit. When he saw that there was not enough wood to finish cooking it, he called Harlequin and Punchinello and said :

" Bring me the marionette which you will find hanging on a nail. He is made of nice, dry wood, and will make a fine fire for my roast."

At first Harlequin and Punchinello hesitated ; but the Showman glared at them menacingly, and they obeyed. In a few moments they returned to the kitchen carrying poor Pinocchio, who was squirming like an eel out of water, and shrieking desperately : " O Daddy, save me ! I don't want to die ! I don't want to die ! "

CHAPTER ELEVEN

Fire-Eater Sneezes and Forgives Pinocchio, and Pinocchio Later Saves the Life of his Friend Harlequin

FIRE-EATER (this was the Showman's name) appeared to be a frightful man, there's no doubt about it, with that black beard hanging down like an apron, quite covering his chest and legs, but at heart he was really not so bad. When he saw poor Pinocchio struggling and screaming, " I don't want to die ! I don't want to die ! " he began to feel sorry for him, and although he tried to prevent it, at last he could resist no longer, but sneezed with all his might.

Harlequin had been looking as dejected and sorrowful as a weeping willow, but when he heard that sneeze his face grew brighter, and bending towards Pinocchio he whispered :

" Good news, brother. The Showman has sneezed. That's a sign that he is sorry for you. You are saved."

For you must know that while other men weep, or at least wipe their eyes when they are sorry for someone, whenever Fire-Eater really pitied anyone, he had the habit of sneezing. Perhaps it's as good a way as any other to show one's kindness of heart.

After the Showman had sneezed, he continued to speak gruffly, and shouted at Pinocchio :

" Stop that crying ! It gives me an uncomfortable feeling in the pit of my stomach . . . I feel such a pain that . . . that . . . a-tchoo ! a-tchoo ! "—and this time he sneezed twice.

" Long life to you ! " said Pinocchio.

" Thank you. And your father and mother, are they still alive ? " asked Fire-Eater.

" My father is, but I never knew my mother."

" How sorry your old father would be if I should throw you on the fire ! Poor old man ! I pity him ! A-tchoo ! a-tchoo ! a-tchoo ! "—and he sneezed three times.

"Long life to you!" cried Pinocchio to Fire-Eater.

"Thank you. On the other hand you should be sorry for me, because, as you see, I haven't wood enough to finish roasting my supper; and my word for it, you certainly would have been very handy. But now I have spared you, and I must make the best of it. I will put some marionette of my Company under the spit in your stead. Olà, police!"

Two wooden policemen appeared immediately in response to this command. They were very tall, and very thin. They wore policemen's helmets, and carried drawn swords in their hands.

The showman said in a hoarse voice:

"Take that Harlequin, bind him tightly and throw him on the fire. My mutton must be well roasted!"

Imagine poor Harlequin! He was so terrified that his legs doubled up under him, and he fell forward on his face.

At that melancholy sight Pinocchio threw himself at the Showman's feet and, weeping such quantities of tears that the whole length of his long beard was drenched, he cried in an imploring voice:

"Have mercy, Signor Fire-Eater!"

"There are no signori here!" replied the Showman sternly.

"Have mercy, Cavalier!"

"There are no Cavaliers here!"

"Have mercy, Commander!"

"There are no Commanders here!"

"Have mercy, Your Excellency!"

When he heard himself called "Your Excellency," the Showman pursed up his lips, and, suddenly becoming more human and tractable, he said to Pinocchio:

"Well, what can I do for you?"

"I implore you to spare poor Harlequin!"

"It is useless to ask for that. If I spare you, I must put him on the fire, for my mutton must be well roasted.

"In that case," cried Pinocchio, rising to his feet, and throwing away his cap of bread, "in that case I know my duty. Forward, police! Bind me and throw me in the fire. It is not just that poor Harlequin, my own true friend, should die for me ! "

These words, uttered in a loud, heroic voice, caused all the marionettes who were present to weep. Even the policemen, although made of wood, cried like babies.

At first Fire-Eater remained as hard and cold as a piece of ice : then, little by little, he began to melt, and to sneeze. When he had sneezed four or five times, he opened his arms affectionately to Pinocchio, saying :

" You are a fine, brave boy ! Come here, and give me a kiss."

Pinocchio ran quickly, and, climbing up the Showman's beard like a squirrel, gave him a resounding smack on the end of his nose.

" And is my life spared ? " asked poor Harlequin, in a trembling voice that could hardly be heard.

" Your life is spared," replied Fire-Eater ; then he added, as he shook his head : " Patience ! This evening I must resign myself to eat my mutton half done ; but another time woe to him who must help roast it ! "

When they knew that their brothers were safe, all the marionettes ran back to the stage, lit all the lights as for a grand performance, and began to skip and dance. They were still dancing at sunrise.

Chapter Twelve

Fire-Eater Gives Pinocchio Five Gold Pieces to Take to his Father, Geppetto : but Pinocchio is Deceived by the Fox and the Cat and Goes away with them

The next day Fire-Eater called Pinocchio aside and asked him :

" What is your father's name ? "

" Geppetto."

" And what trade does he follow ? "

" That of a poor man."

" Does he earn very much ? "

" He earns as much as is necessary in order never to have a farthing in his pocket. Just think of it ! In order to buy my primer so that I could go to school, he had to sell the coat off his back : a coat that was full of holes and patches ! "

" Poor fellow ! I am almost sorry for him. Here are five gold pieces. Go quickly and give them to him with my compliments."

As one can easily imagine, Pinocchio thanked the Showman a thousand times. One by one he embraced all the marionettes of the Company, and even the policemen ; then, almost beside himself with joy, he set out for home.

But before he had travelled half a mile he met a Fox who was lame in one foot, and a Cat who was blind in both eyes, hobbling along as well as they could, like good companions in misfortune. The Fox, who was lame, was leaning on the Cat : and the Cat, who was blind, was guided by the Fox.

" Good morning, Pinocchio," said the Fox politely.

" How is it that you know my name ? " asked the marionette.

" I know your father well."

" Where did you see him ? "

" I saw him yesterday in the doorway of his house."

" And what was he doing ? "

" He was in his shirt-sleeves, and trembling with cold."

" Poor Daddy ! But, thank Heaven, from this day forth he shall tremble no more."

" Why not ? "

" Because I have become a rich man."

" You ? A rich man ? " said the Fox, and he began to laugh scornfully. The Cat laughed, too, but he stroked his whiskers with his fore paws in order to conceal it.

" There's nothing to laugh at," cried Pinocchio irritably. " I'm really sorry to tantalise you, but these, if you understand such things, are five beautiful gold pieces."

And he took the money Fire-Eater had given him from his pocket. At the fascinating jingle of gold the Fox made an involuntary movement of the leg that seemed lame, and the Cat opened wide both his blind eyes ; but he shut them again so quickly that Pinocchio never noticed it.

" And now," inquired the Fox, " what are you going to do with this money ? "

" First of all," answered the marionette, " I am going to buy a fine new coat for my father ; a coat made of gold and silver, with diamond buttons ; then I will buy myself a primer."

" For yourself ? "

" Certainly : for I mean to go to school and study hard."

" Look at me," said the Fox ; " because of my foolish passion for study, I lost the use of my leg."

" And look at me," said the Cat ; " because of *my* foolish passion for study, I lost the sight of both my eyes."

Just then a white blackbird that was sitting on a hedge by the side of the road sang its usual song, and said :

" Pinocchio, don't heed the advice of evil companions : if you do, you'll be sorry."

Poor blackbird, if only he hadn't said it ! The Cat made a great leap right upon him, and, without giving him time to say *ouch*, swallowed him at a mouthful, feathers and all.

When he had devoured him and wiped his mouth, he shut his eyes and became blind as at first.

" Poor blackbird," said Pinocchio ; " why did you treat him so ? "

" I did it to teach him a lesson. He will learn not to interfere again when other people are talking."

They had gone more than half-way towards Pinocchio's home, when the Fox stopped suddenly and said :

" Would you like to double your gold pieces ? Would you like to turn those five miserable gold pieces into a hundred, a thousand, two thousand ? "

" *Would* I ? But how can it be done ? "

" It's the easiest thing in the world. Instead of going home, you must come with us."

" And where are you going ? "

" We are going to Dupeland."

Pinocchio thought a moment, and then said resolutely :

" No, I don't want to go. I am almost home, and I want to go to my father, who is waiting for me. Who knows how he must have worried when I didn't come home ! I know only too well that I have been a very bad boy. The Talking Cricket was right when he said : ' Disobedient children will never be happy in this world.' I have proved it to my cost, for I have suffered all sorts of misfortunes ; and last night, in Fire-Eater's house, I was in danger of . . . Brrr ! It gives me goose-flesh to think of it."

" Well, then," said the Fox, " so you really want to go home ? Run along then, and so much the worse for you ! "

" So much the worse for you ! " repeated the Cat.

" Think well, Pinocchio, because you're turning your back on a fortune ! "

" On a fortune ! " repeated the Cat.

" Your five gold pieces might become two thousand in one day ! "

" Two thousand in one day ! " repeated the cat.

" But how could they possibly become so many ? " demanded Pinocchio, with his mouth wide open in astonishment.

" I will explain immediately," said the Fox.

" You must know that in Dupeland there is a sacred field called ' The Field of Miracles.' You dig a little hole in this field, and you put in it, for example, a gold sequin. Then you cover it up with earth, water it with two buckets of spring water, sprinkle a pinch of salt over it, and go peacefully to bed. During the night the sequin sprouts and blossoms and the next morning you get up, go back to the field, and what do you find ? You find a lovely tree, loaded with as many gold sequins as an ear of corn has kernels."

" Then," said Pinocchio, more bewildered than ever, " if I should bury my five gold pieces in that field how many should I find the next morning ? "

" That's a very easy problem," replied the Fox, " a problem that can be done on one's fingers. Suppose that every gold piece becomes a cluster of five hundred gold pieces ; multiply five hundred by five, and the next morning you will find in your pocket two thousand five hundred shining, clinking gold pieces."

" Oh, how splendid ! " cried Pinocchio, dancing for joy. " As soon as I have harvested these gold pieces, I will take two thousand for myself, and I will make you two a present of the other five hundred."

" A present—to us ? " exclaimed the Fox disdainfully. " You offend us ! God forbid ! "

" God forbid ! " repeated the Cat.

" What good people ! " thought Pinocchio ; and straightway forgetting his father, the new coat, the primer, and all his good resolutions, he said to the Fox and the Cat :

" Well, lead on, I will go with you."

CHAPTER THIRTEEN

The Red Crab Inn

THEY walked, and walked, and walked, and finally towards evening, tired almost to death, they arrived at the Red Crab Inn.

" Let us stop here a little while," said the Fox, " at least long enough to eat a bite, and rest a few hours. At midnight we must go on again, so that we can arrive at The Field of Miracles by sunrise."

They entered the Inn and sat down at a table, but none of them had any appetite.

The poor Cat had a bad stomach-ache, and could only eat thirty-five mullett in tomato sauce, and four helpings of tripe with Parmesan cheese ; and because he thought the tripe was not well seasoned, he asked three times for more butter and grated cheese.

The Fox, too, would gladly have nibbled something, but since the doctor had put him on a diet he had to be content with a hare in sweet-sour sauce, with a light border of fat spring chickens. After the hare, in order to stimulate his appetite, he asked for a dish of pheasants, partridges, rabbits, frogs, lizards, and paradise grapes. After this he would not touch anything more. He said he was so sick of the sight of food that he could not eat another mouthful.

The one who ate least of all was Pinocchio. He asked for a quarter of a nut, and the small end of a loaf of bread, but he left it all on his plate. The poor child's thoughts were fixed on The Field of Miracles, and he was suffering from a prospective indigestion of gold pieces.

When they had supped, the Fox said to their host :

" Give us two nice rooms : one for Signor Pinocchio, and the other for me and my companion. We will take a little nap before we leave. Do not forget to call us at midnight, for we must continue our journey."

" Yes, sir," replied the host, winking at the Fox and the Cat as if to say : " I understand what you are up to."

As soon as he was in bed, Pinocchio fell soundly asleep, and began to dream. He thought that he was in the middle of a field, and the field was full of little trees whose branches were loaded with gold pieces swinging gently in the breeze, and clinking as if to say : " Whoever wants us, come and get us." But just at the most interesting point, that is, when Pinocchio stretched out his hand to gather them and put them in his pocket, he was suddenly awakened by three violent blows on the door of his room.

It was the host, come to tell him that it was midnight.

" Are my companions ready ? " asked the marionette.

" Ready ! They left two hours ago."

" Why were they in such a hurry ? "

" Because the Cat received a message that his eldest son, who has chilblains, is not expected to live."

" Did they pay for their supper ? "

" What an idea ! They were far too polite to offer such an insult to a gentleman like you."

" That's too bad ! Such an insult would have been most welcome ! " said Pinocchio, scratching his head. Then he inquired :

" And where did these good friends of mine say they would wait for me ? "

" In The Field of Miracles, to-morrow morning, at sunrise."

Pinocchio parted with a gold piece for his supper, and that of his fellow travellers, and left the Inn.

He had to feel his way, for it was so dark it was impossible to see one's hand before one's face. In the country round him not a leaf could be heard stirring. Only a few night birds, flying across the path from one hedge to the other, brushed Pinocchio's nose with their wings, making him start backwards in a fright, crying : " Who goes there ? " an echo answered from the far-off hills : " Who goes there ? Who goes there ? Who goes there ? "

As he trudged along he saw a little animal on the trunk of a tree, which shone with a pale, faint light, like a night lamp with a porcelain shade.

" Who are you ? " asked Pinocchio.

" I am the ghost of the Talking Cricket," was the reply in a faint, faint voice, that seemed to come from another world.

" What do you want of me ? " said the marionette.

" I want to give you some advice. Go back home, and carry the four gold pieces you have left to your poor father, who is weeping and longing for you."

" My father will be a rich gentleman to-morrow, for these four gold pieces will have become two thousand."

" My boy, never put your faith in people who promise to make you rich in a day. They are generally swindlers, or crazy. Listen to me, and go back home."

" No, I am going forward."

" It is very late."

" I am going forward."

" It is a dark night."

" I am going forward."

" And it's a dangerous way . . ."

" I am going forward."

" Remember that children who do as they please are sorry for it sooner or later."

" That's an old story. Good night, Cricket ! "

" Good night, Pinocchio ; may Heaven preserve you from fogs and assassins ! "

With these words the Talking Cricket's light went out, as when one blows out a candle, and the path was darker than before.

Chapter Fourteen

Pinocchio does not Heed the Good Advice of the Talking Cricket, and Meets the Assassins

" REALLY," said the marionette to himself, as he continued his journey, " how unfortunate we poor children are ! Everybody scolds us, everybody warns us, everybody advises us. To hear them talk you would think they were all our fathers, or our schoolmasters—every one of them : even the Talking Crickets. The ideas! Just because I would not listen to that tiresome Talking Cricket, who knows, according to him, how many disasters will befall me ! I shall even encounter assassins ! It's a good thing I don't believe, and never have believed, in assassins. I am perfectly certain that assassins have been invented by our fathers on purpose to frighten us, so that we shall be afraid to go out at night. And even supposing I should meet them, would I be afraid of them ? Not for a moment ! I should walk right up to them and say : ' Mr. Assassins, what do you want of me ? Just bear in mind that there's no joking with me. Now be quiet, and go about your business ! ' If those poor assassins should hear me talking like that, I can just see them running off like the wind. If it should happen, though, that they didn't run away, *I* should, and that would be the end of it."

Pinocchio was going to say something more, but at that moment he thought he heard a rustling of leaves behind him.

Turning quickly he saw two horrid black figures wrapped in coal sacks leaping towards him on their toes, like two spectres.

" There they are, for sure ! " he said to himself, and not knowing where to hide his four gold pieces he put them in his mouth, under his tongue.

Then he started to run ; but before he had taken the first step he felt himself seized by his arms, and heard two horrible, cavernous voices behind him.

"Your money, or your life!" the terrible voices cried.

Pinocchio couldn't speak, for his money was in his mouth. He made a thousand bows and gestures to show those masked robbers, of whom he could only see their eyes through the holes in the sacks, that he was a poor man, and hadn't even a counterfeit penny in his pocket.

"Come, come, less nonsense, and hand over your money!" the two brigands cried menacingly.

But the marionette made signs with his head and hands as if to say: "I have not a penny!"

"Hand over your money, or you are a dead man," said the tall assassin.

"A dead man!" repeated the other.

"And after we have killed you, we will kill your father too!"

"Your father, too!" repeated the other.

"No, no, no, my poor father, no!" cried Pinocchio in despair; but at this the gold pieces clinked in his mouth.

"Ah, ha, you rascal, so you hid your money under your tongue! Spit it out, immediately!"

Pinocchio paid no attention.

"Oh! so you don't understand? Wait a moment, we'll make you spit it out!"

In fact one of them seized the marionette by the end of his nose, and the other grasped his chin, and they pulled without mercy, one this way, and the other that way, in order to make him open his mouth, but it was no use; the marionette's mouth was as tightly shut as if it had been nailed and riveted.

Then the smaller assassin drew a knife, and tried to force it between his lips, but Pinocchio, quick as lightning, bit off his hand. Imagine his astonishment when he saw that it was a cat's paw!

Encouraged by this first victory, he freed himself from the assassins' clutches and, jumping over the hedge, fled across the country with the assassins after him, like dogs after a hare. The smaller one, who had lost a paw, ran on one leg, though how he managed it was never known.

After they had run about nine miles, Pinocchio was completely exhausted. Seeing himself lost, he climbed a tall pine tree, and seated himself on a branch at the very top. The assassins tried to climb up after him, but half-way up the trunk they slipped and fell to the ground, skinning their hands and feet.

In spite of this they did not give up, but, gathering a heap of dry sticks at the foot of the tree, they set fire to it. In less than no time the pine caught fire, and blazed like a candle in the wind. Pinocchio, seeing that the flames were climbing fast, and not wanting to be roasted like a pigeon, leaped down from his perch and took to his legs again across the fields and vineyards. The assassins followed after, running close behind him, never seeming to be tired at all.

It was nearly daybreak and they were still running, when suddenly Pinocchio found the way barred by a wide, deep ditch full of dirty water, the colour of coffee and milk. What should he do? "One, two, three!" cried the marionette, and dashing forward like the wind he jumped clean over it. The assassins jumped too, but they had not gauged the distance properly and swash, spatter! they fell right in the middle of the ditch.

Pinocchio heard the splash, and as he ran he laughed, and shouted :

"Take a good bath, Mr. Assassins!"

He was just thinking that they must be drowned when, turning to look, he saw them both running after him, still wrapped in their sacks, and dripping like two leaky baskets.

CHAPTER FIFTEEN

The Assassins Follow Pinocchio, and having Caught him they Hang him on the Big Oak Tree

THIS time the marionette felt that his case was hopeless. He was ready to throw himself to the ground and surrender when his eyes fell upon a little house, as white as snow, far off among the dark green trees.

" If only I have breath enough left to get to that house, perhaps I should be safe," he said to himself.

Without losing a moment he ran towards the grove at his best speed, with the assassins hot on his track.

After a desperate run, which lasted nearly two hours, he arrived at last, completely worn out, at the door of the little house.

He rapped; but no one answered.

He rapped again, louder than before, for he heard the footsteps and the panting breath of his persecutors; but all was silent as before.

Seeing that it was useless to rap, he began to kick the door, and beat his head against it. At that a lovely child came to the window. Her hair was blue, and her face as white as wax; her eyes were closed, and her hands were crossed on her breast. Without moving her lips in the least she said in a low voice that seemed to come from another world:

" There is no one in this house. They are all dead."

" But at least you will let me in," cried Pinocchio, weeping and entreating her.

" I am dead, too."

" Dead ? Then what are you doing at the window ? "

" I am waiting for the hearse to come, and take me away."

As she said this the child disappeared, and the window closed of itself, silently.

" Oh, lovely blue-haired child," implored Pinocchio, " open the door, for pity's sake. Have mercy on a poor boy who is pursued by assass . . ."

But before he could finish the word he felt himself seized by the neck, and heard those cruel voices snarling :

" This time you won't escape us ! "

The marionette felt that his end was near, and he began to tremble. He shook so violently that the joints of his wooden legs creaked, and the four gold pieces under his tongue clinked together.

" Now, then," demanded the assassins, " will you, or will you not open your mouth ? You won't answer, eh ? Well, leave it to us : we'll see that you open it this time ! "

And drawing two great knives as sharp as razors, zaff . . . they struck at him savagely. Luckily for him the marionette was made of the hardest kind of wood ; and the knife blades were splintered into a thousand pieces. Only the handles remained in the assassins' hands, who stood staring at each other in amazement.

" I see," said one, " he must be hung. Let us hang him ! "
" Let us hang him ! " repeated the other.

No sooner said than done. They bound his hands behind his back, and, putting a running noose around his neck, they tied him to a branch of a big oak tree.

Then they sat on the grass, and waited for him to stop kicking ; but after three hours the marionette's eyes were wide open, and he was kicking harder than ever.

At last, tired of waiting, they turned to Pinocchio and said with a sneer :

" Good-bye, until to-morrow. We will come back then, and we hope you will be so obliging as to see that we find you good and dead, and with your mouth wide open."

Then they went away.

Meanwhile a fierce north wind had begun to blow ; it raged, and whistled, and blew poor Pinocchio back and forth as fast as a bell-clapper on a holiday It hurt him dreadfully, and the noose tightened around his neck so that he could not breathe.

Little by little his eyes grew dim, and although he felt that death was near, still he hoped that some kind soul might come that way and release him. He waited and waited, but no one came, no one at all. Then he remembered his poor father, and he stammered, half dead as he was :

"O Daddy ! If you were only here ! "

He could say no more. He closed his eyes, opened his mouth, stretched out his legs, shuddered all over, and became as stiff as if he were frozen.

CHAPTER SIXTEEN

The Lovely Blue-Haired Child Saves the Marionette : she Puts him in Bed and Calls Three Doctors to See whether he is Alive or Dead

WHILE poor Pinocchio, hung by assassins on the big oak tree, seemed more dead than alive, the lovely child with blue hair looked out of the window again. She felt very sorry for the unlucky marionette who, hanging by his neck, was dancing to the tune played by the cold north wind. She clapped her hands three times, making a faint sound.

At this signal there was a rustling as of hurrying wings, and a large Falcon appeared and perched on the window-sill.

"What are your commands, beautiful Fairy?" said the Falcon, lowering his beak in homage (for you must know that the child with blue hair was no other than a kind fairy, who had lived in the neighbourhood of that grove for more than a thousand years).

"Do you see that marionette hanging on the big oak?"

"I see him."

"Very well; fly there quickly; break the knot that holds him with your strong beak, and lay him gently on the ground at the foot of the oak."

The Falcon flew away, and in two minutes he returned, saying:

"Your commands have been obeyed."

"How did you find him? Alive or dead?"

"To look at him he seems dead, but he cannot be quite dead, for as soon as I loosened the noose around his neck, he sighed and murmured: 'Now I feel better!'"

The Fairy clapped her hands twice, and a magnificent poodle appeared, walking upright on his hind legs, as if he were a man. The Poodle was dressed like a coachman on a holiday. He had a

57

little three-cornered hat trimmed with gold braid, a white curly wig, a chocolate-coloured doublet with diamond buttons and two big pockets for the bones which his mistress gave him at dinner, short trousers of crimson velvet, silk stockings, low shoes, and a sort of umbrella case behind, made of blue satin, to put his tail in when it rained.

" Be quick, Medora ! " said the Fairy ; " get out my finest carriage and drive to the grove. When you come to the big oak you will find a poor, half-dead marionette lying on the ground. Take him up carefully, put him gently on the cushions, and bring him to me. Do you understand ? "

The Poodle wagged the blue satin case he carried behind him three or four times to show that he understood, and was off like a shot.

In a few moments a handsome carriage was driven out of the stable. It was the colour of air, and was padded with canary feathers and lined with whipped cream and custard, with sweet cakes. It was drawn by a hundred pairs of white mice, and the Poodle on the box cracked his whip over their heads like a cab-driver afraid of being late.

In less than a quarter of an hour he was back again. The Fairy, who was waiting at the door, took the poor marionette in her arms, carried him to a little chamber with mother-of-pearl walls, and sent instantly for the most famous doctors in the neighbourhood.

The doctors came hurrying, one after another : there were a Crow, an Owl, and a Talking Cricket.

" I would like these gentlemen to tell me," said the Fairy, as they stood around Pinocchio's bed, " I would like these gentlemen to tell me if this unfortunate marionette is dead or alive."

The Crow came forward first, and felt Pinocchio's pulse ; then he felt his nose, and lastly his little toe. When he had examined them carefully he said with great solemnity :

" It is my opinion that this marionette is quite dead ; but if, unluckily, he is not dead, that would be a sure sign that he is still alive."

" I am sorry," said the Owl, " to contradict the Crow, my illustrious friend and colleague, but it is my opinion that this marionette is still alive ; but if, unluckily, he is not alive, that would be a sign that he is actually dead."

" And have you nothing to say ? " inquired the Fairy, turning to the Talking Cricket.

" I think that when a prudent physician does not know what to say, the best thing he can do is to be silent. As for that, this marionette's features are not new to me ; I have seen him before."

Pinocchio, who until that instant had seemed as lifeless as a genuine piece of wood, gave a convulsive shudder that shook the whole bed.

" That marionette there," continued the Talking Cricket, " is an accomplished rogue . . ."

Pinocchio opened his eyes, but closed them quickly.

" He is a scamp, a shirker, a vagabond . . ."

Pinocchio hid his face under the sheet.

" That marionette is a disobedient son, who will cause his poor old father to die of a broken heart ! "

Just then a smothered sobbing and weeping could be heard in the room. Imagine how surprised every one was when they lifted up the sheet a little, and saw that Pinocchio was the cause of it.

" When a bad boy weeps, it's a sign that he is on the way to recovery," said the Crow solemnly.

" I am sorry to contradict my illustrious friend and colleague," said the Owl, " but it's my opinion that in such a case it is a sign that he does not want to die."

CHAPTER SEVENTEEN

Pinocchio Eats the Sugar, but is not Willing to Take the Medicine: however, when he Sees the Grave-Diggers Coming to Carry him away he Swallows it : then he Tells a Lie and his Nose Grows Longer by Way of Punishment

As soon as the three doctors had left the room, the Fairy came to his bedside. She put her hand on Pinocchio's forehead, and saw that he had a burning fever.

So she dissolved a white powder in half a glass of water, and holding it to his lips said affectionately :

" Drink this, and in a few days you will be well."

Pinocchio looked at the glass, pursed up his lips, and said in a whining voice :

" Is it sweet, or bitter ? "

" It is bitter, but it will do you good."

" If it's bitter I don't want it."

" Listen to me, and drink it."

" But I don't like anything bitter."

" Drink it, and afterwards I will give you a lump of sugar, to take the taste out of your mouth."

" Where is the lump of sugar ? "

" Here it is," said the Fairy, taking one out of a golden sugar bowl.

" First I want the lump of sugar, and then I'll drink that bitter water."

" Will you promise to drink it ? "

" Yes."

The Fairy gave him the sugar, and Pinocchio crunched and swallowed it in an instant, saying as he picked his fingers :

" It would be pretty fine if sugar were medicine. I would be sick every day."

" Now keep your promise, and drink these few drops of water ; they will make you well."

Pinocchio took the glass in his hand most unwillingly. He sniffed at it, and held it to his lips ; then he sniffed again, and at last he said :

" It's too bitter ! It's too bitter ! I can't drink it ! "

" How can you say so, when you haven't even tasted it ! "

" Oh, I know it is ! I can smell it. Give me another lump of sugar, and then I'll drink it."

So the Fairy, with all the patience of a kind mother, put another lump of sugar in his mouth : then she offered him the glass.

" I can't drink it this way," said the marionette, making all sorts of grimaces.

" Why not ? "

" Because that pillow on my feet makes me so uncomfortable." The Fairy removed the pillow.

" It's no use, I can't drink it this way, either."

" Whatever is the matter now ? "

" The door bothers me, it's half open."

The Fairy shut the door.

" In fact," cried Pinocchio, bursting into tears, " I don't want to drink that bitter water, no, no, no . . ."

" My child, you will be sorry."

" I don't care."

" You are very ill."

" I don't care."

" This fever will send you to the other world in a few hours."

" I don't care."

" Are you not afraid to die ? "

" Not a bit ! I had rather die than drink that dreadful medicine ! "

At that very moment the door of the room was thrown open, and four rabbits black as ink came in, carrying a little black coffin.

" What do you want of me ? " screamed Pinocchio, sitting up in terror.

" We have come for you," said the largest rabbit.

" For me ! But I'm not dead yet ! "

"Not quite yet, but you have only a few minutes to live, because you refused to drink the medicine that would have cured you."

"O Fairy, kind Fairy," cried Pinocchio, "give me the glass quickly . . . hurry, for mercy's sake, for I don't want to die, no, I don't want to die!"

He took the glass in both hands, and emptied it at one gulp.

"Patience!" said the rabbits. "This time we have made a trip for nothing."

And replacing the little coffin on their shoulders they went out of the room, muttering and grumbling through their teeth.

In a few minutes Pinocchio jumped out of bed perfectly well; for you must know that wooden marionettes have the privilege of being ill very seldom, and of getting well very quickly.

When the Fairy saw him running and playing around the room as gay as a young rooster, she said:

"So my medicine really did do you good?"

"More than that! It brought me back to the world."

"Then why was it so much trouble to make you drink it?"

"Well, we children are all like that. We are more afraid of the medicine than of the disease."

"For shame! Children should know that the right medicine taken in time may save them from a serious illness, perhaps even from death."

"Oh, another time I will not make so much trouble. I will remember those black rabbits with the coffin on their shoulders and I'll take the glass in my hand instantly, and down it will go!"

"Now come here to me, and tell me how it happened that you fell into the hands of assassins."

"It was like this: Fire-Eater, the Showman, gave me some gold pieces and said: 'Here, take these to your father.' But on the way I met the Fox and the Cat, two very nice persons, and they said: 'Would you like to change these pieces into a thousand, yes, two thousand? Come with us, and we will take you to The Field of Miracles.' So I said: 'Let us go'; and they said: 'Let's stop at the Red Crab Inn, and set out again after midnight.' And when I woke up they were not there, because they had gone away. Then I started after them in the night. It seemed impossible that it could be so dark, and I met two assassins in coal sacks, who said : ' Hand over your money ! ' And I said, ' I haven't any,' because I had hid the four gold pieces in my mouth. One of the assassins tried to put his hand in my mouth, and I bit it off, but when I spat it out it wasn't a hand, but a cat's paw. And the assassins ran after me, and I ran and ran as fast as I could go until they caught up with me, and hung me by the neck to a tree in the grove saying : ' We will come back to-morrow, and then you will be dead, and your mouth will be open, and we can get the money which is under your tongue.' "

" Where are the four gold pieces now ? " asked the Fairy.

" I have lost them," replied Pinocchio, but he told a lie, for he had them in his pocket.

As soon as he had told this lie his nose, which was already very long, became two inches longer.

" Where did you lose them ? "

" In the grove nearby."

At this second lie, his nose became still longer.

" If you lost them there," said the Fairy, " we can go and find them ; for everything that is lost in that grove can be found."

" Oh ! Now that I remember," replied the marionette in great confusion, " I didn't lose the money, I swallowed it when I was taking your medicine."

At this third lie his nose lengthened to such an extraordinary degree that poor Pinocchio could not move in any direction. If he turned one way, his nose hit the bed or the window-panes ; if he turned the other, it struck the walls or the door ; if he raised it a little more, there was danger of putting out the Fairy's eye.

The Fairy watched him, and laughed.

" What are you laughing at ? " asked the marionette, much embarrassed and worried about that nose, which was growing while he looked at it.

" I am laughing at the lies you have told, little Pinocchio."

" However did you know that I told lies ? "

" Lies, my child, can be easily recognised. There are two sorts of them : those with short legs, and those with long noses. The sort you tell have long noses."

Pinocchio would have hidden his face for shame. He tried to run out of the room, but he could not do it ; his nose was so long that he could not reach the door.

CHAPTER EIGHTEEN

Pinocchio Finds the Fox and the Cat and Goes with them to Sow the Four Gold Pieces in the Field of Miracles

As you may, perhaps, imagine, the Fairy let the marionette scream and cry a good half-hour because he could not get to the door on account of his long nose. She did this to teach him a good lesson, and to cure him of the bad habit of lying, which is one of the worst habits a boy can have. But when she saw his face swollen with crying, and his eyes starting out of his head in his despair, she was moved to pity and clapped her hands. At that signal a thousand big wood-peckers flew in at the window, and perching on Pinocchio's nose pecked away at it so industriously that in a few minutes his enormous, ridiculous nose was reduced to its natural size again.

" How kind you are, dear Fairy," said the marionette, wiping his eyes. " I love you so much ! "

" I love you too," replied the Fairy, " and if you will stay with me you shall be my little brother, and I will be your loving sister."

" I would love to stay with you . . . but what about my poor father ? "

" I have thought of everything. Your father knows all about you, and he will be here before night."

" Really ? " exclaimed Pinocchio, jumping for joy. " Then, dear Fairy, if you are willing, I would like to go to meet him. I can't wait to see that poor old man, who has suffered so much for me ! "

" Go, by all means, but don't get lost. Take the path through the grove, and you will be sure to meet him."

Pinocchio departed ; and as soon as he entered the grove he began to run like a deer. At a certain point just in front of the old oak he stopped, because he thought he heard something moving in the bushes. In fact, there appeared all at once in the path—can you guess?—the Fox and the Cat, his two travelling companions, with whom he had supped at the Red Crab Inn.

" Here is our dear Pinocchio," exclaimed the Fox, hugging and kissing him. " How do you happen to be here? "

" How do you happen to be here? " repeated the Cat.

" It's a long story," said the the marionette. " I will tell it when I have time, although you should know that the other night when you left me alone in the Inn, I encountered assassins on the way."

" Assassins? Oh, my poor friend! And what did they want? "

" They wanted to rob me of my money."

" Infamous! " said the Fox.

" Most infamous! " added the Cat.

" But I began to run," continued the marionette, " and they ran after me until they caught me, and hung me to a branch of that oak."

And Pinocchio pointed to the big oak nearby.

" Did you ever hear of anything worse than that! " said the Fox. " What a world this is, in which we are condemned to live! Where can honest men like us find a refuge? "

While they were talking Pinocchio noticed that the Cat was lame in his right foreleg, because the whole paw was missing. He therefore said to him:

" What has become of your paw? "

The Cat started to say something, but he began to stammer— and the Fox said quickly:

" My friend is too modest; that is why he doesn't answer. I will reply for him. You know, about an hour ago we met an old wolf, who was almost dying of hunger. He begged us for a crust of bread, but we hadn't even a fishbone to give him; so what do you suppose my friend here did, he who has the heart of a Caesar? He bit off his own paw and gave it to that poor beast, so that he could break his fast."

As he said this, the Fox wiped away a tear.

Pinocchio's heart was so touched by this story that he went

close to the Cat, and whispered in his ear : " If all cats were like you, the rats would be fortunate ! "

" And what are you doing here ? " asked the Fox.

" I'm waiting for my father ; he may be here any moment."

" And your gold pieces ? "

" They are all in my pocket, except the one I spent at the Red Crab Inn."

" Just to think that instead of four gold pieces they might be a thousand, or two thousand by to-morrow ! Why not take my advice ? Why not plant them in The Field of Miracles ? "

" Impossible, to-day ; I will go some other time."

" Another time will be too late," said the Fox.

" Why ? "

" Because a rich man has bought the field, and after to-morrow no one will be allowed to plant his money there."

" How far is it to The Field of Miracles ? "

" Only a little over a mile. Will you come with us ? You will be there in half an hour ; you can sow your four gold pieces immediately, and after a few minutes you can gather two thousand and come home in the evening with your pockets full. Will you come ? "

Pinocchio hesitated ; he remembered the good Fairy, old Geppetto, and the warnings of the Talking Cricket ; but he finished by doing as all children do who have no judgment, and no heart : that is to say, he tossed his head and said to the Fox and the Cat :

" Come on : I'll go with you."

And off they went.

They had walked about half a day when they came to a place called Zanytrap. As soon as they entered the city, Pinocchio saw that the streets were full of dogs whose hair had fallen off, and whose mouths were wide open with hunger ; there were shorn sheep, trembling with cold ; chickens without their crests and wattles, who were begging for a grain of corn ; big butterflies who could not fly, because they had sold their beautiful wings; peacocks without their tails, who were ashamed to be seen ; and pheasants who were slinking along, mourning for their lovely gold and silver feathers, which were lost for ever.

In the midst of this throng of beggars and shamefaced beasts, elegant carriages rolled by now and then, with a Fox, or a thievish magpie, or some bird of prey inside.

" But where is The Field of Miracles ? " inquired Pinocchio.

" Just a few steps farther on."

They traversed the city, and, going beyond the walls, stopped in a lonely field which, by the way, was just like any other field.

" Here we are," said the Fox. " Now get down and dig a little hole with your hands, to put your gold pieces in."

Pinocchio obeyed. He dug the hole, put in the four gold pieces he had left, and covered them up.

" Now, then," said the Fox, " go to the mill-dam close by, get a bucket of water, and water the ground where you have sown your seed."

Pinocchio went to the mill-dam, and, since he did not have a bucket, he took off one of his shoes, filled it with water, and watered the earth which covered his money.

" What else must I do ? "

" Nothing more," replied the Fox. " Now you can go away. Come back in about twenty minutes, and you will find a little tree already growing, with its branches covered with money."

The poor marionette was almost beside himself with joy. He thanked the Fox and the Cat a thousand times, and promised them a fine present.

" We don't want presents," replied those two miserable wretches ; " it is enough for us to have shown you how to get rich without work. That makes us perfectly happy "

With these words they wished Pinocchio a splendid harvest, bade him farewell, and went about their business.

CHAPTER NINETEEN

*Pinocchio Loses his Gold Pieces and Spends Four Months in
Prison*

THE marionette went back to the city, and began to count the
minutes, one by one. When he thought he had waited twenty
minutes, he hurried back to The Field of Miracles.

He went as fast as he could, while his heart beat like a clock,
tick, tock, tick, tock, and he said to himself :

" What if, instead of a thousand gold pieces, I should find
two thousand on the branches of the tree ? Or instead of two
thousand, I should find five thousand ? Or instead of five thousand, one hundred thousand ? Oh, what a grand gentleman I
should be then ! I should have a splendid palace, and a thousand
wooden horses and a thousand stables to play with, and a
cellar full of toffee, and lemonade, and a library just full of
candied fruit, and tarts, and sweet rolls, and almond paste,
and lollipops, and cream puffs ! "

While he was indulging in these fancies, he came within sight
of the field. He stopped to see if he could catch a glimpse of
a tree, with its branches laden with money, but he saw nothing.
He went a little farther, still nothing. He entered the field,
went up to the place were he had buried his gold pieces, and
there was nothing at all. He stood there thinking ; and,
forgetting the rules of etiquette, he took one hand out of his
pocket, and scratched his head vigorously.

At that moment a loud laugh rang in his ears. Looking up
he saw a large parrot on the branch of a tree, picking the
lice off the few feathers he had left.

" Why are you laughing ? " said Pinocchio peevishly.

- " I am laughing because, in cleaning my feathers, I tickled
myself under my wings."

The marionette did not reply. He went to the mill-dam,

filled his shoe with water again, and poured it on the earth which covered his money.

But lo, another laugh, more impertinent than before, rang out over the lonely field.

" See here," shouted Pinocchio angrily, " might one ask what you are laughing at, you ill-mannered parrot ? "

" I am laughing at those simpletons who believe all the nonsense they are told, and who are always cheated by those who are more cunning than themselves."

" Are you, perhaps, speaking of me ? "

" Yes, poor Pinocchio, I am speaking of you, of you who are so simple as to believe that you can sow and reap money, like beans and pumpkins. There was a time when I believed that, too, and to-day I am suffering for it. To-day (alas ! too late) I have learned that to get a little money together honestly, you must know how to earn it by the labour of your hands or your head."

" I don't understand," said the marionette, beginning to tremble with fear.

" Patience ! I will try to speak plainer," replied the Parrot. " While you were in the city the Fox and the Cat came back here ; they dug up your money and ran away like the wind. It will take a swift runner to catch them."

Pinocchio stood there with his mouth wide open. He could not believe what the Parrot said, and he began wildly to dig up the earth he had watered He dug, and dug, and dug, until he had a hole big enough for a haystack, but the money was not there.

Then in desperation he ran back to the city, and went straight to the Court House, to denounce the villains who had robbed him.

The Judge was an old Gorilla. He was very old, and presented a most respectable appearance, with his long white beard, and his gold spectacles without any glass in them, which he was obliged to wear all the time on account of a disease of the eyes which he had had for many years.

In the Judge's presence Pinocchio related all the circumstances of the iniquitous fraud, of which he had been the victim. He gave the names, surnames, and all the particulars concerning the rascals, and finished by demanding justice.

The Judge listened benevolently, for he was greatly interested in his story, and very sorry for him. When the marionette had no more to say, he put out his hand and rang a bell.

At the sound two mastiffs appeared, dressed like policemen. The Judge pointed to Pinocchio and said :

" This poor fellow has been robbed of four gold pieces. Take him to prison immediately."

Pinocchio was thunderstruck. Such a sentence as this was like a flash of lightning out of a clear sky. He was about to protest, but the policemen didn't want to waste any time, so they clapped their paws over his mouth, and took him to gaol.

And there he stayed for four months ; four long months, and it would have been longer if it had not happened, luckily, that the young Emperor of Zanytrap, having won a glorious victory over his enemies, commanded a great public rejoicing. There were illuminations, fireworks, horse and bicycle races, and, best of all, he ordered the prisons to be thrown open, and all the rascals to be set free.

" If the others leave the prison, I want to go too," said Pinocchio to the gaoler.

" Oh, no, you can't leave," replied the gaoler, " for you are not in that class."

" I beg your pardon," said Pinocchio, " I am a rascal too."

" In that case, you are perfectly right," said the gaoler, and lifting his cap respectfully he made a low bow, opened the prison door, and let him pass.

CHAPTER TWENTY

When Pinocchio is Liberated from Prison he Starts for the
Fairy's House, but on the Way he Meets with a Horrible
Serpent, and Afterwards is Caught in a Trap

IMAGINE Pinocchio's joy when he was free once more ! Without losing a moment he hurried out of the city, and took the street that led to the Fairy's little house.

It had been raining, and the mud was so deep that it came half-way up his legs ; but he paid no attention to it. He was so anxious to see his father, and his little blue-haired sister, that he ran and jumped like a greyhound, and the mud spattered as high as his head. As he ran he said to himself :

" What dreadful misfortunes have befallen me ! . . . and I deserve them, too. I always want my own way, and never listen to those who love me, and who have a thousand times more judgment that I have ! But from this time forward I will lead a different life, and become a sensible, obedient boy ; for I have seen by this time that disobedient children always get the worst of it, and never gain anything by having their own way. I wonder if my father is waiting for me ? Shall I find him at the Fairy's house ? It's so long since I have seen him that I cannot wait to throw my arms around his neck and kiss him. Will the Fairy forgive me for disobeying her ? What good care she took of me, and how kind she was ! If I'm alive to-day it's all owing to her ! Was there ever a boy more ungrateful and heartless than I am ? "

As he said this he stopped suddenly in fright, and stepped backwards quickly.

What had he seen ?

He saw a great Serpent stretched across the way. His skin was green, his eyes were like fire, and smoke was coming from his pointed tail as if from a chimney.

Words fail me to express Pinocchio's terror. He went back a quarter of a mile, and sat down on a little heap of stones to wait until the Serpent should go about his business, and leave the road free for him to pass.

He waited an hour; two hours; three hours; but the Serpent was still there, and even from where he sat he could see his fiery eyes, and the column of smoke coming out of his tail.

At last Pinocchio summoned all his courage, and coming near the Serpent he said, in a very small, sweet, insinuating voice:

"Excuse me, Mr. Serpent, but would you be so kind as to move just a little, barely enough to let me pass?"

He might just as well have spoken to a wall. There was no reply.

He began again, with that same small voice:

"You must know, Mr. Serpent, that I am going home, where my father is waiting for me, and it's so long since I have seen him! Would you be willing for me to go on my way?"

He waited for some sign in reply to his request, but no sign came. Instead, the Serpent, who had until then seemed full of life, became perfectly quiet and rigid. He closed his eyes, and his tail stopped smoking.

"Perhaps he is really dead," said Pinocchio, rubbing his hands together for joy, and without waiting another second he was about to step over him. But just as he was lifting one leg the Serpent rose up suddenly like a watch spring, and the marionette in his fright leaped backwards so quickly that he stumbled and fell.

It was truly a bad fall, for he came down with his head sticking in the mud, and his legs up in the air.

At the sight of the marionette standing on his head in the mud, and kicking faster than any marionette had ever kicked before, the Serpent was seized with a fit of laughter. He laughed, and he laughed, and he laughed, until he burst a blood vessel, and this time he was dead for good.

And now Pinocchio began to run again as fast as he could, in order to reach the Fairy's house before dark. But he became so dreadfully hungry that he jumped over a hedge to pick a few bunches of grapes. If only he had not done so !

He had barely reached the vines, when—*crack !* he felt his legs gripped by two sharp irons : the pain was so terrible that he saw all the stars there were in the sky.

The poor marionette was caught in a trap put there to catch some large polecats that had been terrorising all the henhouses in the neighbourhood.

CHAPTER TWENTY-ONE

Pinocchio is Captured by a Farmer who Makes him Act as a Watchdog for his Henhouse

As you can easily imagine, Pinocchio began to scream and cry and call for help; but it was perfectly useless, for there were no houses to be seen, and not a living soul passed by.

Meanwhile night came on.

Pinocchio was almost fainting: partly on account of the pain caused by the irons which cut into his shin, and partly because he was afraid, there all alone in the dark, in the midst of the fields. Seeing a firefly above his head, he called to him:

" O, little Firefly, won't you be so merciful as to deliver me from this torment ? "

" Poor boy ! " replied the Firefly, gazing at him compassionately. " How did you ever get caught in the grip of those sharp irons ? "

" I came into the field to pick a few bunches of grapes and . . ."

" But are they your grapes ? "

" No . . ."

" And who ever taught you to take things that do not belong to you ? "

" I was hungry . . ."

" Hunger, my child, is not a good excuse for taking what does not belong to you."

" That's true, that's true," wailed Pinocchio, " I won't do it again."

This dialogue was interrupted by the sound of footsteps drawing near. It was the owner of the field, who was coming on tiptoe to see if he had caught one of those polecats that were eating his chickens at night.

When he drew his lantern from under his coat he was amazed to see that, instead of a polecat, he had caught a boy.

" Ah, you thief ! " the farmer said angrily, " so it's you who are stealing my chickens ! "

" It isn't me, it isn't me," sobbed Pinocchio ; " I only came into the field to pick a few bunches of grapes ! "

" Anyone who will steal grapes will steal chickens. Leave it to me ! I'll teach you a lesson you'll remember for a while !"

He opened the trap, seized the marionette by the collar, and lugged him off under his arm as he would have carried a lamb.

When he reached the yard in front of his house, he threw Pinocchio on the ground, and putting one foot on his neck he said :

" It's late, and I want to go to bed. I will settle with you to-morrow. Meanwhile, since my watchdog died to-day, you may take his place. You shall be my watchdog."

So saying he put a heavy collar covered with sharp brass studs around his neck, and fastened it so tightly that it was impossible to slip his head through it. A long iron chain was attached to the collar, and fixed firmly to the wall.

" If it should rain to-night," said the farmer, " you may crawl into that little wooden kennel. The straw there has served for four years as a bed for my poor dog. Remember to keep your ears pricked up and, if, unluckily, thieves should come, don't forget to bark."

With this last caution the farmer went into the house and locked the door, leaving poor Pinocchio crouching in the yard, more dead than alive with hunger and fright. From time to time he thrust his fingers under the collar which pinched his throat, and exclaimed, weeping :

" It serves me right ! It serves me perfectly right ! I wanted to be a loafer and a vagabond. . . . I listened to evil companions, and as a consequence I always have bad luck. If I had only been a good boy, like so many others, if I had been willing to work and study, if I had stayed at home with my poor father,

I would not be now away out here in this lonely place, acting as a watchdog for a farmer. Oh, if I could only be born again ! But it's too late, now, I must have patience ! "

This sorrowful plaint, which came from the bottom of his heart, relieved him a little. He crawled into the kennel, and went to sleep.

CHAPTER TWENTY-TWO

Pinocchio Discovers the Thieves and is Set Free as a Reward for his Fidelity

HE had been sleeping soundly for more than two hours, when about midnight he was awakened by a whispering and muttering of strange voices that seemed to come from the yard. He put the point of his nose out of his kennel and saw four animals with dark fur, talking together. They looked like cats, but they were not cats. They were polecats, carnivorous animals that are especially fond of eggs and young chickens. One of them left his companions, and coming to the door of the kennel said in a low tone :

" Good evening, Melampo."

" My name is not Melampo," said the marionette.

" Who are you, then ? "

" I am Pinocchio."

" And what are you doing there ? "

" I am a watchdog."

" But where is Melampo ? Where is the old dog that lived in this kennel ? "

" He died this morning."

" Died ? Poor beast ! He was so kind ! However, judging by your countenance, you seem to be a good-natured dog."

" Excuse me, I am not a dog ! "

" Ah ! What are you, then ? "

" I am a marionette."

" And you act as a watchdog ? "

" Alas, yes : it's for a punishment ! "

" Well, I'll make the same bargain with you that I made with old Melampo ; I'm sure you will be satisfied."

" And what might that be ? "

" We will come to the henhouse one night a week, as in the

past, and carry off eight hens. We will eat seven, and give you one, on condition, you understand, that you pretend to sleep when we come, and never bark and wake up the farmer."

" Is that what Melampo did ? "

" Yes, indeed, and we always got on splendidly together. Now sleep in peace, and be sure that before we leave we will bring you a chicken, already picked, for to-morrow. Do you understand ? "

" I understand only too well," replied Pinocchio, shaking his head menacingly, as if he would have preferred to say : " We'll see about that pretty soon ! "

When the four polecats felt sure of their safety, they went straight to the henhouse, which was close to the kennel. They tore open the little wooden door with their teeth and claws, and slipped inside, one after the other. But no sooner were they all inside when the little door closed with a loud bang.

It was Pinocchio who had closed it, and not content with this, he put a big stone against it for greater security.

Then he began to bark, and he barked just like a watchdog : " Bow-wow-wow-wow ! "

When the farmer heard him barking, he jumped out of his bed, seized his gun, and raising the window, he called out :

" What's the matter ? "

" The thieves are here ! " cried Pinocchio.

" Where are they ? "

" In the henhouse ! " replied Pinocchio.

" I am coming immediately."

In less time than you can say " Jack Robinson " the farmer appeared. He ran to the henhouse, and after catching the four polecats and popping them into a sack he exclaimed in high glee :

" At last you have fallen into my hands ! I might chastise you, but I am not so cruel. I will therefore satisfy myself by taking you to the landlord in the village, who will skin you and cook you in a sweet-sour sauce, and serve you for rabbit. It is an honour you do not deserve, but generous people like me do not mind doing such good turns."

Then he went to Pinocchio, caressed and praised him, and asked him among other questions :

"How did you discover the plot of these thieves ? To think that Melampo, my faithful Melampo, never suspected anything !"

The marionette could have revealed the truth ; that is he could have told the farmer of the shameful bargain between the dog and the polecats ; but he remembered that the dog was dead, and he said to himself : "What good will it do to accuse the dead ? Since they are dead and gone, the best way is to leave them in peace."

"Were you awake, or asleep, when the polecats first appeared ?" inquired the farmer.

"I was asleep," replied Pinocchio, "but they woke me by talking together, and one of them even came to my kennel, and said : 'If you will promise not to bark and wake up the farmer, we will give you a chicken, already picked.' What do you think of that ? The impudence of making such a proposal to me ! I am a marionette, and I know I am full of faults, but I would never plot with thieves, nor receive stolen goods !"

"Good for you, my boy," said the farmer, patting him on the back. "Such sentiments do you honour ; and to show how pleased I am with you I will set you free, and you may go home."

And he took off the dog collar.

CHAPTER TWENTY-THREE

Pinocchio Weeps for the Death of the Lovely Blue-Haired Child: then he Finds a Dove who Carries him to the Seashore where he Throws himself into the Water to Save his Father

When Pinocchio no longer felt the weight of that heavy, humiliating collar on his neck, he began to run across the fields, never stopping for a moment, until he reached the highway which led to the Fairy's house.

When he reached it he paused to look down on the surrounding country. He could see plainly, with the naked eye, the site of his unlucky encounter with the Fox and the Cat : he could see the grove with the big oak on which he had been hanged, rising high above the other trees : but although he looked in all directions, he could not discover the little white house where he had found the lovely blue-haired child.

Fearing he knew not what, he took to his heels, and ran with all his might and main. In a few minutes he found himself in the field where the little white house once stood. But the little house was no longer there. Instead there was a little slab of white marble on which these sad words were inscribed :

HERE LIES
THE BLUE-HAIRED CHILD
WHO DIED OF GRIEF
ON BEING ABANDONED BY HER
LITTLE BROTHER
PINOCCHIO

I leave you to imagine the marionette's feelings when he had spelled out these words. He fell to the ground, and kissing the cold marble a thousand times, he burst into a flood of tears. He wept all that night, and at daybreak he was still weeping, although his tears were all spent. His groans and lamentations were so loud and piercing that they were echoed from all the hills around him.

As he wept he said :

" O dear Fairy, why are you dead ? Why am I not dead, who am so naughty, instead of you, who were so good ? And my father, where is he ? O dear Fairy, tell me where I can find him, for I want to stay with him always, and never, never, never leave him. Dear Fairy, tell me it is not true ; that you are not dead ! If you really love me, if you love your little brother, live once more, come back as you were before ! Are you not sorry to see me here alone, abandoned by everyone ? If the assassins come, they will hang me again, and then I should be dead for good. What will become of me, alone in the world ? Now that I have lost you and my father, who will give me something to eat ? Where will I sleep ? Who will make me a new jacket ? Oh, better a hundred times better, that I should die too ! Yes, I want to die ! Boo-hoo-hoo ! "

While he was in this desperate state he tried to tear out his hair, but since it was of wood he couldn't even run his fingers through it.

At this moment a very large dove, that was flying high in the air above him, stopped short with outstretched wings, and cried :

" Tell me, child, what are you doing down there ? "

" Don't you see ? I'm crying ! " said Pinocchio, turning up his face towards the voice, and rubbing his eyes with the sleeve of his jacket.

" Tell me," continued the dove, " do you happen to know among your playmates a marionette called Pinocchio ? "

" Pinocchio ? Did you say Pinocchio ? " cried the marionette, jumping to his feet. " I'm Pinocchio ! "

At this reply the dove dropped swiftly to the ground. He was larger than a turkey.

" Do you know Geppetto ? " he asked of the marionette.

" Do I know him ? He is my poor father ! Has he spoken to you of me ? Will you take me to him ? Is he still alive ? "

" I left him three days ago on the sea coast."

" What was he doing ? " Pinocchio asked the large dove.

" He was making a little boat in which to cross the ocean. That poor man ! It is more than four months that he has been wandering around the world looking for you. Not having found you he has taken it into his head to search for you in far-off countries across the sea."

" How far is it from here to the sea coast ? " Pinocchio inquired anxiously.

" More than five hundred miles."

" More than five hundred miles ? O dear Dove, what a fine thing it would be if I had your wings ! "

" If you want to go I will carry you."

" How ? "

" Astride my back. Are you very heavy ? "

" Heavy ? No, indeed ! I'm as light as a feather."

Without another word Pinocchio jumped on the Dove's back, with a leg on each side of him like a real horseman, and cried joyfully : " Gallop, gallop, little horse, for I'm in such a hurry ! "

The Dove took flight, and in a few minutes he was so high up that he almost touched the clouds. Arrived at that great height the marionette was seized with curiosity, and he looked down at the world below him ; but it frightened him, and made him so dizzy that he wound his arms tight around the neck of his feathered steed to keep from falling off.

They flew all day. Towards evening the Dove said :

" I am so thirsty."

" And I am so hungry ! " added Pinocchio.

" Let us stop a few minutes at this dovecote ; then we will continue our journey, and by sunrise we shall be at the sea coast."

They entered a deserted dovecote where they saw only a basin of water, and a basket full of lettuce.

The Marionette had never in his life been able to eat lettuce. He always said it turned his stomach ; but that evening he simply devoured it, and when it was all gone he said to the Dove :

" I never would have believed that lettuce could taste so good ! "

" You will learn, my boy," replied the Dove, " that when you are actually hungry, and there is nothing else to eat, even lettuce seems delicious. Hunger is never particular or finicky."

After this little snack they did not wait to rest themselves, but hurried on their way, and the next morning they were at the seashore.

The Dove stopped just long enough for Pinocchio to dismount, and then flew away immediately, to avoid being thanked for having performed a kindness.

The beach was covered with people who were shouting and gesticulating as they looked out over the ocean.

" What is the matter ? " Pinocchio inquired of a little old woman.

" A poor father has lost his son, and he was going to cross the sea in a little boat to look for him, but the waves are so high that the boat will be capsized."

" Where is the boat ? "

" Right there, in front of my finger," said the old woman, pointing to a little boat which at that distance looked like a nutshell with a tiny man in it.

Pinocchio looked closely, and uttered a piercing shriek :

" It's my father ! It's my father ! "

Meanwhile the little boat, beaten by the angry waves, now disappeared entirely, and again could be seen on the crest of a wave. Pinocchio, standing on a high rock, called his father's name over and over, making signs with his hands, and waving his cap and handkerchief.

Although Geppetto was so far away, it seemed as if he recognised his son, for he took off his cap and waved it : he also made signs as if he would gladly return to land, but the sea was so furious that he could not use his oars.

Suddenly there came a mighty wave, and the little boat disappeared. They waited to see it afloat once more, but they never saw it again.

" The poor man ! " said the fishermen who were gathered on

the beach ; and murmuring a prayer they turned to go to their homes.

Suddenly there was a desperate shout, and turning to look they saw a boy throw himself into the sea from the top of a high rock, crying:

" I will save my father ! "

Pinocchio, being made of wood, floated easily and swam like a fish. They saw him disappear under the water, and reappear to be beaten about by the waves. Now a leg appeared, now an arm at a great distance from land, and at last they lost sight of him altogether.

" Poor boy ! " said the fishermen who were gathered on the beach; and murmuring a prayer they went back to their homes.

Chapter Twenty-Four

Pinocchio Arrives at Busy-Bee Island and Finds the Fairy

INSPIRED by the hope of arriving in time to save his poor father, Pinocchio swam all that night.

And what a terrible night it was! Floods of rain, hailstones, fearful thunderclaps, and flashes of lightning that made the world as bright as day.

Towards morning he saw not far off a long strip of land. It was an island in the midst of the ocean.

He put forth every effort to reach the shore, but all in vain. The tumbling waves tossed him back and forth as if he were straw or chaff. At last, luckily for him, there came a monstrous wave which picked him up and threw him violently on the beach.

He struck the earth so hard that all his ribs and joints rattled ; but he comforted himself by saying :

" That was another narrow escape ! "

Little by little the clouds disappeared, the sun shone forth in all his splendour, and the sea became as smooth as oil.

The marionette spread his clothes to dry in the sun, and began to look in every direction over that immense waste of waters to see if there was anywhere a tiny boat with a little man in it. But although he looked and looked he saw only the sky and the sea, and the sails of some ships, so far away that they looked like flies.

" If I only knew the name of this island ! " he said. " If I only knew whether it is inhabited by well-bred people, who are not in the habit of hanging boys on trees ! Is there no one of whom I could inquire ? "

The idea of being alone, all alone in an uninhabited country made him so melancholy that he was just going to cry when he saw a large fish close to the shore, swimming along about his business, with his head out of water.

Since he did not know his name, he cried as loud as he could :

" Hallo, Mr. Fish, may I say a word to you ? "

" Two of them," replied the fish, who was such a very polite dolphin that there were few like him in all the seas of the world.

" Will you be so kind as to tell me if there are places in this island where one may eat, without danger of being eaten ? "

" Certainly there are," replied the Dolphin ; " there is one only a short distance from here."

" Which way shall I take to go there ? "

" Take that little path on your left, and follow your nose. You can't make a mistake."

" Tell me something more. You swim in the sea all day and all night: have you, perchance, seen a little boat with my father in it ? "

" Who is your father ? "

" He is the best father in the world ; and I am the worst possible son."

" Considering the storm we had last night," said the Dolphin, " his boat was probably sunk."

" And my father ? "

" By this time he must have been eaten by the terrible shark that has been spreading death and destruction in these waters for a long time."

" Is he very big, this shark ? " inquired Pinocchio, trembling with fright.

" *Is* he ! " exclaimed the Dolphin. " Well, just to give you an idea, I will say that he is larger than a five-storey house, and his mouth is so wide and deep that it would easily hold a railway train, engine and all."

" Heavens above ! " cried the terrified marionette and, hurrying into his clothes, he turned to the Dolphin saying : " Good-bye, Mr. Fish, pardon the trouble I have caused you, and a thousand thanks."

With these words he almost ran down the little path. At the least sound he turned quickly to look behind him, fearing to see that horrible shark as large as a five-storey house, and with a railway train in his mouth, coming after him.

He had travelled about half an hour when he came to Busy-Beeville. The streets were full of people hurrying back and forth on business, everybody had something to attend to; everybody was working; you could not have found an idler or a vagrant if you had searched with a lantern.

" I see," said that lazybones of a Pinocchio to himself, " this place will never do for me. I was not born to work."

By this time he was suffering dreadfully from hunger, for he had had nothing to eat for more than twenty-four hours, not even a dish of lettuce.

What could he do ?

There were only two ways of getting something to eat : to ask for work, or to beg for a few pennies or a bit of bread.

He was ashamed to beg. His father had always taught him that only the aged and helpless have a right to beg. The poor in this world, those who really deserve to be helped and pitied, are those who by reason of old age or sickness are no longer able to earn their bread by their own labour. It is the duty of all others to work ; and if they refuse to do so, and suffer hunger, so much the worse for them.

While Pinocchio hesitated, a man passed by, perspiring and panting, who was pulling alone, and with great difficulty, two carts loaded with coal.

Pinocchio judged by his countenance that he was a kind man ; so he went up to him, and, casting his eyes downwards in shame, he said in a low tone :

" Will you please give me a penny, for I am dying of hunger."

" Not only one penny," replied the coal dealer, " but I will give you four, if you will help me to draw these loads of coal home."

" I wonder at you ! " exclaimed the marionette indignantly. " Allow me to inform you that I am not a donkey ! "

" The better for you ! " replied the coal dealer. " Then, my boy, if you are really dying of hunger, eat a couple of slices of your pride, and be careful not to have indigestion."

After a few minutes a bricklayer passed by, carrying a hod of cement on his shoulder.

" Kind sir, would you be so generous as to give a penny to a poor boy who is starving ? "

" Willingly : come with me and carry cement," replied the bricklayer, " and instead of one penny, I will give you five."

" But cement is so heavy," objected Pinocchio, " and I don't want to work."

" If you don't want to work, my boy, amuse yourself by being hungry, and much good may it do you."

In less than half an hour twenty people passed by, and Pinocchio begged of every one of them, but they all replied :

" Aren't you ashamed ! Instead of begging on the street, go to work, and earn your bread ! "

At last a kind little woman appeared carrying two pitchers of water.

" Kind lady, will you let me have a sip of water from your pitcher ? " asked Pinocchio, who was burning with thirst.

" Yes, drink, my child," said the little woman, putting the pitchers on the ground.

When Pinocchio was as full as a sponge, he wiped his mouth and grumbled :

" Now I'm no longer thirsty ! If I were only no longer hungry ! "

When the good little woman heard these words she said quickly :

" If you will carry one of these pitchers home for me, I will give you a large slice of bread."

Pinocchio looked at the pitcher, and said neither yes nor no.

" And with the bread I will give you a fine dish of cauliflower, seasoned with oil and vinegar," the good woman added.

Pinocchio looked at the pitcher again, but he did not say yes or no.

" And after the cauliflower I will give you some delicious pastry."

At this last temptation Pinocchio could resist no longer ; he drew a long breath and said resolutely :

" Patience ! I will carry the pitcher home for you."

The pitcher was very heavy, and the marionette's hands not being strong enough to hold it, he had to set it on his head.

When they arrived at her home the good woman placed Pinocchio at a little table already set, and put the bread, the cauliflower, and the pastry before him.

Pinocchio did not eat like a human being, but rather like a pig. His stomach was like a house that has been empty and tenantless for months.

Little by little the worst pangs of his hunger were appeased, and he raised his head to thank his benefactress. No sooner had he looked at her than he uttered a long " O-o-o-oh ! " of astonishment, and sat as if turned to stone, with his eyes starting from his head, his fork in the air, and his mouth full of bread and cauliflower.

" Whatever is the matter with you ? " said the good woman, laughing.

" It's because . . ." stammered Pinocchio, " it's because . . . because . . . you are like . . . you remind me of . . . yes, yes, the same voice . . . the same eyes . . . . the same hair . . . you have blue hair, too, just like her ! O dear Fairy, O dear Fairy, tell me, is it you? Is it really you? Don't make me cry any more ! If you only knew ! I have cried so much, I have suffered so much ! "

As he said this, Pinocchio wept floods of tears and, falling on his knees before her, he threw his arms about that mysterious little woman.

CHAPTER TWENTY-FIVE

*Pinocchio Promises the Fairy that he will be Good and Study,
Because he is Tired of being a Marionette and Wants to Become
a Real Boy*

AT first the little woman would not admit that she was the
Fairy with the blue hair ; but seeing that she had been recognised, and not wishing to continue the comedy any longer, she
revealed herself, saying to Pinocchio :

" You rogue of a marionette, how did you recognise me ? "

" It's because I love you so much that I knew you."

" Do you remember ? I was a little girl when you left me,
and now I am a woman. I could almost be your mother."

" I should like that so much ; then instead of calling you
my little sister, I could call you mamma. I have always wished
that I had a mother like other boys ! But how did you manage
to grow so quickly ? "

" That's a secret."

" Teach it to me : I would like to be a little bigger. Just look
at me ! I have never been more than knee-high."

" But you can't grow," replied the Fairy.

" Why not ? "

" Because marionettes never grow. They are born marionettes, they live marionettes, and they die marionettes."

" I am sick to death of always being a marionette ! " cried
Pinocchio, striking his wooden head. " It's about time I
became a man, like other men ! "

" If only you deserved it, you could become one."

" Truly ? And what can I do to be worthy of becoming a
man ? "

" It's very easy : you begin by being a good boy."

" Oh ! do you mean to say that I am not a good boy ? "

" You are anything but a good boy ! Good boys are obedient,
and you . . ."

91

" I am never obedient," Pinocchio said to the Fairy.

" Good boys like to work and study, and you . . ."

" And I am a blockhead and a vagrant all the year round."

" Good boys always tell the truth . . ."

" And I always tell lies."

" Good boys like to go to school . . ."

" And school gives me a pain. But from this day forward I will lead a different life."

" Will you promise to do so ? "

" Yes, I promise. I want to become a good boy, too, and be the consolation of my father. Where can my poor father be now ? "

" I don't know."

" Will I ever be so fortunate as to see him again ? "

" I hope so ; yes, I am sure of it."

Pinocchio was so happy when he heard this that he grasped the Fairy's hands and kissed them, almost crazy with joy. Then looking up at her affectionately, he said :

" Tell me, Mamma, it wasn't true, then, that you were dead ? "

" It seems not," replied the Fairy with a smile.

" If you only knew how sad I felt and how my heart ached when I read, HERE LIES . . ."

" I know, and that is why I forgave you. You were truly sorry, and then I knew that you had a good heart ; and if a child has a good heart, even if he is mischievous and brought up badly, one can always hope that he will mend his ways. That is why I came here to look for you. I will be your mamma . . ."

" Oh, how splendid ! " cried Pinocchio, jumping for joy.

" You will always obey me, and do as you are told."

" Oh, yes, yes, yes ! "

" To-morrow," added the Fairy, " you will begin by going to school."

Pinocchio became a little less joyful.

" Then you will choose some profession or trade, whichever you would like . . ."

Pinocchio looked straight at the Fairy and made a wry face.

" What are you muttering between your teeth ? " inquired the Fairy indignantly.

" I was saying," grumbled Pinocchio, " that it seems to me it's too late now for me to go to school."

" No, indeed ! Bear this well in mind : that it's never too late to study and get an education."

" But I don't want to learn any profession or trade . . ."

" Why not ? "

" Because I don't like work."

" My child," said the Fairy, " those who talk in that way generally finish in a hospital, or in a prison. Remember this : that whether a man is born rich or poor, it is his duty to find something to do in this world ; to busy himself about something. Woe to those who idle their time away ! Idleness is a dreadful disease, of which one should be cured while still a child ; if not, one never gets over it."

These words touched Pinocchio's heart. He lifted his head quickly and said to the Fairy :

" I will study, I will work. I will do everything you want me to, for I am sick of leading the life of a marionette. I want to become a real boy, cost what it may. You promised that I could, didn't you ? "

" Yes, I promised, and now it depends on you."

CHAPTER TWENTY-SIX

Pinocchio Goes to the Seashore with his Schoolmates to See the Terrible Shark

THE very next day Pinocchio went to school. Imagine what those mischievous children did when they saw a marionette coming to school ! They laughed as if they would never stop. First one and then another played some trick on him. They snatched his cap out of his hand, and pulled his jacket from behind. They tried to make a big moustache under his nose with ink, and finally they tried to tie strings to his hands and feet to make him dance.

Pinocchio pretended not to notice them at first, and attended to his own business; but at last he lost his patience, and turning on the worst of his tormentors he exclaimed menacingly:

" Be careful, boys ! I didn't come here to play the clown for you. I respect others, and I want to be respected."

" Good for you, scallywag ! You talk just like a book ! " shouted the rogues, doubling up with laughter ; and one of them, more impertinent than the rest, put out his hand to seize the marionette by the nose.

But he was not quick enough, for Pinocchio kicked his shins under the table.

" Oh, oh ! what hard feet ! " cried the boy, rubbing his aching shins.

" And what elbows ! They're harder than his feet ! " exclaimed another who had received a blow in the pit of his stomach in return for his unkind jokes.

After a few of these proofs of his ability to defend himself, Pinocchio won the esteem and goodwill of the whole school, and they became very fond of him.

Even the Master praised him, because he was attentive, studious, and intelligent. He was always the first at school, and the last to rise from his desk when school was out.

His only fault was that he made too many friends, and some of them were only too well known as scapegraces, who were unwilling to study. The Master warned him daily, and the kind Fairy never failed to say over and over :

" Be careful, Pinocchio, those bad schoolmates of yours will end by making you cease to love your books ; they may even get you into great trouble."

" Oh, there's no danger ! " replied the marionette, shrugging his shoulders and touching his forehead with his finger as if to say : " There's so much good sense inside ! "

Now it happened one day as he was on his way to school that he met some of these companions of his, who said :

" Have you heard the great news ? "

" No."

" They say there's a shark in the sea as big as a mountain."

" Is it possible ! What if it should be the same shark that I heard of the night my poor father was drowned ? "

" We're going to the beach to see it. Won't you come too ? "

" Not I ! I want to go to school."

" What do you care for school ? We can go to school to-morrow. What's one lesson more or less ? We shall still be the same blockheads."

" But what will the Master say ? "

" Let him say what he likes. That's what he is paid for, to find fault all the time."

" And my mamma ? "

" Oh, she'll never find out ! " replied those wicked boys.

" I know what I'll do," said Pinocchio ; " I have certain reasons for wanting to see the shark, but I'll go to see him after school."

" You poor simpleton ! " retorted one of the boys, " do you suppose a fish of that size will wait until you are ready to call on him ? When he's tired of being in one place, he whisks away to another, and good night ! "

" How long will it take to go to the beach ? " asked the marionette.

" We can go and come back in an hour."

" Well, come on then, he who runs fastest is the best fellow ! " cried Pinocchio.

At this declaration all those scamps ran off across the fields with their books and slates under their arms. Pinocchio was at their head; he ran as if he had wings on his feet.

From time to time he turned to tease his companions, who were a long way behind him ; and when he saw them panting, exhausted, covered with dust, and with their tongues hanging out, he laughed heartily. The unhappy boy little knew at that moment what terrors and what dreadful disasters awaited him.

CHAPTER TWENTY-SEVEN

There is a Great Battle between Pinocchio and his Companions during which One of them is Wounded and Pinocchio is Arrested

WHEN he arrived at the seashore, Pinocchio looked quickly around, but he saw no shark. The sea was as smooth as a great mirror.

" Well, where's the shark ? " he inquired, turning to his companions.

" Perhaps he has gone to breakfast," said one of them, laughing.

" Or perhaps he has gone to bed to take a nap," said another, laughing still louder.

Their silly answers and stupid laughter showed Pinocchio that it was all a practical joke, and that they had told him something that was not true. He was very angry, and he said indignantly :

" And now ? Did you have any object in telling me that story about the shark ? "

" Indeed we did ! " the rogues replied in chorus.

" Well, what was it ? "

" We wanted you to run away from school, and come with us. Aren't you ashamed to be so punctual and studious every day ? Aren't you ashamed to study so hard ? "

" And what business is it of yours how hard I study ? "

" It certainly is our business, for you make us cut a sorry figure before the Master."

" Why ? "

" Because boys who study always make those who don't, like us, cut a poor figure; and we don't like to cut a poor figure. We have some pride, too."

" What can I do then to satisfy you ? "

" You must do as we do, and hate the school, and the lessons, and the Master : our three greatest enemies."

" And suppose I choose to keep on studying at school ? "

" Then we will have nothing more to do with you, and at the very first chance we'll get even with you ! "

" Really, you make me laugh," said the marionette, shaking his head.

" Be careful, Pinocchio," said one of the largest boys, walking towards him. " Don't think you can bully us ; don't think you can crow over us. If you aren't afraid of us, we're not afraid of you. Remember that you are alone, and there's seven of us ! "

" Seven, like the mortal sins," exclaimed Pinocchio, laughing boldly.

" Did you hear that? He has insulted all of us. He has called us the seven mortal sins ! "

" Pinocchio, beg our pardon, or it will be the worse for you ! "

" Coo-coo ! " said the marionette, tapping his nose with his forefinger, derisively.

" Pinocchio, you'll be sorry ! "

" Coo-coo ! "

" We'll beat you like a dog ! "

" Coo-coo ! "

" You'll go home with a broken nose ! "

" Coo-coo ! "

" I'll give you ' Coo-coo ! ' " cried the most daring of those bullies ; " take this on account, and keep it for supper."

With this, he gave him a blow on the head.

But it was, as we say, charge and counter-charge, for the marionette, as was to be expected, replied with another blow, and in a moment the combat became general and furious.

Although Pinocchio was alone, he defended himself like a hero. His hard wooden feet worked so fast that his enemies were kept at a respectful distance. Wherever those feet touched they left a black-and-blue mark that would not be soon forgotten.

Then these bad boys, angry because they could not get near Pinocchio, began to throw things at him. They unstrapped their schoolbooks, and began to throw their primers and grammars and other schoolbooks. But the marionette's sharp eyes kept such a good look-out, and he dodged so quickly, that the books all flew over his head into the sea.

What do you suppose the fishes did ? They thought those books were something to eat, and they came to the surface in shoals ; but no sooner had they tasted a page or two, or a frontispiece, than they spat it out again with a grimace which seemed to say : " We are accustomed to much better food than this ! "

The battle was growing more furious when suddenly a large Crab that had crawled out of the water up on to the beach croaked loudly in voice like that of a trombone with a cold :

" Stop it, you rascals ! These schoolboys' battles always end badly. Someone is sure to be injured ! "

Poor old Crab ! He might as well have preached to the wind. Indeed that imp of a Pinocchio scowled back at him, and said rudely : " Shut up, you detestable Crab ! You had much better be taking some lozenges to cure the cold in your throat. Go to bed, now, and take a sweat ! "

Just then the boys, who had thrown away all their own, saw the marionette's books lying on the ground, and in less time than it takes to tell it they took possession of them.

Among these books there was a large one bound in paper, with sheepskin back and corners. It was a " Treatise on Arithmetic." I leave you to imagine how heavy it must have been !

One of these rogues seized this volume, and aiming at Pinocchio's head, he let it fly with all the force he could muster : but instead of hitting the marionette it struck one of his companions on the head. The child turned as white as a sheet, and crying out, " Oh, Mamma, help me, I am dying ! " he fell his full length on the sandy beach.

At that, the frightened boys took to their legs, and in a few moments they were out of sight.

But Pinocchio remained there, and although he was more

dead than alive himself from sorrow and fright, he ran a wet handkerchief in the sea, and put it on the poor boy's temples, while he wept bitterly, calling him by name, and saying :

" Eugene, poor Eugene ! Open your eyes and look at me ! Why don't you answer me ? It was not I who hurt you so ! Believe me, it was not I ! Open your eyes, Eugene. If you keep them closed, I shall die too. Alas ! alas ! how can I go back home ? How can I have the courage to go back to my mother ? What will become of me ? Where shall I fly ? Where can I hide myself ? Oh, better, a thousand times better, if I had gone to school ! Why did I listen to evil companions ? They will be my ruin ! The Master told me so, and my mother said the same thing : ' Beware of evil companions ! ' But I am headstrong . . . and obstinate . . . I listen to all they say . . . and then do as I please ! And afterwards I have to pay for it. It has been like that ever since I was born. I was never good for a quarter of an hour at a time. Oh, dear, oh, dear, what will become of me ? "

Pinocchio was still crying, and moaning, striking himself on the head, and calling Eugene, when suddenly he heard footsteps approaching.

He turned. There were two policemen.

" What are you doing there on the ground ? " they demanded.

" I was helping my schoolmate."

" Is anything the matter with him ? "

" I think so."

" I should think so, indeed ! " said one of the policemen, bending over Eugene and looking at him closely. " This boy is wounded on the temple ; who has done this ? "

" Not I," stammered Pinocchio, who was so frightened he could hardly breathe.

" If it was not you, who was it, then ? "

" Not I," repeated Pinocchio.

" With what was he wounded ? "

" With this book."

The marionette picked up the " Treatise on Arithmetic "

bound in paper and sheepskin, and showed it to the policeman.

" Whose book is this ? "

" Mine."

" That's enough. I don't need to know anything more. Get up quickly, and come with us."

" But I . . ."

" Come along ! "

" But I am innocent . . ."

" Come along ! "

Before leaving the spot the policemen called some fishermen who were rowing by close to the shore, and said to them :

" We will leave this wounded boy with you. Take him home and care for him. We will come back to-morrow."

Then they turned to Pinocchio, and placing him between them they said in military accents : " Forward ! and step lively ! If you don't so much the worse for you ! "

Without waiting for them to repeat it, the marionette started down the path that led to the village. The poor fellow did not know whether he was awake or dreaming ; however, he thought he must be dreaming a dreadful dream. He was almost beside himself with shame and despair. His eyes saw double, his legs trembled under him, his tongue stuck to the roof of his mouth, so that he could not say a word. Yet in the midst of his stupefaction and bewilderment one thought pierced his heart like a sword : the thought that he would have to pass under the kind Fairy's window between two policemen. He would rather have died.

They were just entering the village when a gust of wind blew off Pinocchio's cap, and carried it some ten paces away.

" Will you permit me to go and get my cap ? " asked Pinocchio of the policemen.

" Yes, go, but be quick about it."

The marionette picked up his cap, but instead of placing it on his head, he put it between his teeth, and then began to run with all his might towards the sea. He went as if he had been shot out of a gun.

Seeing that it would be difficult to catch him, the policemen sent a great mastiff after him, that had won the first prize in all the dog races. Pinocchio ran, but the mastiff ran faster. The people all came to the window, or rushed into the street to see the end of that wild race. But they never saw it, for Pinocchio and the mastiff raised such a dust that in a few moments it was not possible to see anything.

CHAPTER TWENTY-EIGHT

Pinocchio is in Danger of being Fried Like a Fish

DURING this desperate race there came a terrible moment when Pinocchio felt himself lost, for you must know that Alidoro (that was the mastiff's name) had almost come up to him.

The marionette could hear the dreadful beast panting close behind him, and he even felt his hot breath.

Luckily, he was by this time, close to the beach, and it was only a few steps to the sea.

As soon as he reached the shore the marionette gave a great leap, just like a frog, and fell far out in the water. Alidoro would have stopped, but he was going so fast that he shot out into the water, too. Unfortunately he did not know how to swim, and he began to paw wildly, trying to keep his nose above water; but the harder he tried, the more he went under.

When he came to the surface his eyes were almost starting out of his head. He barked and yelped:

" I'm drowning ! I'm drowning !"

" Drown then," replied Pinocchio, who was now far away and out of all danger.

" Help me, Pinocchio, save my life !"

At that cry of despair the marionette, who at bottom had a very kind heart, had pity on him, and turning to the dog, he said :

" If I save your life will you promise not to bother me or run after me any more ? "

" I promise ! I promise ! Be quick, for pity's sake ! Another half-minute and I shall be drowned."

Pinocchio hesitated an instant, but, remembering that his father had told him many times, that one never loses by doing a good deed, he swam to Alidoro, and taking him by the tail with both hands, he pulled him safe and sound to dry land.

The poor dog could not stand on his feet. He had drunk, in spite of himself, so much salt water that he was swelled up like a balloon. However, the marionette did not dare to trust him too far, so he thought it might be better to throw himself into the sea again. As he swam away he called to the friend he had rescued :

" Good-bye, Alidoro, a good journey to you, and give my love to the folks at home."

" Good-bye, Pinocchio," replied the dog, " a thousand thanks for saving me from death. You have done me a great kindness, and in this world one good turn deserves another. If you should ever need me, I will not fail you."

Pinocchio continued to swim, but he kept near the shore until at last he thought he had reached a safe place. Looking at the beach he saw a sort of grotto in the rock, from which issued a long column of smoke.

" There must be a fire in that grotto," he said to himself. " So much the better ! I can warm and dry myself . . . and then ? And then we shall see what next ? "

Having made this decision he drew near the rocky shore. But just as he was climbing out, he felt something under the water rising, rising, rising, until it lifted him out on the beach. He tried to run away, but it was too late, for, to his great astonishment, he found himself inside a big net, and in the midst of a multitude of fish of every shape and size, that were flapping and jumping as if they were crazy.

And at the same time he saw, coming out of the grotto, a frightful fisherman, who was so ugly that he looked like some marine monster. Instead of hair, a bush thickly covered with green leaves grew on his head. His skin was green, his eyes were green, and his long beard that almost touched the ground was green. He looked like a great green lizard standing on his hind legs.

When the fisherman had drawn the net out of the sea, he cried joyfully :

" Thank Providence ! I shall have a fine dinner of fish to-day ! "

" It's lucky for me that I'm not a fish," said Pinocchio to himself, plucking up a little courage.

The net full of fish was carried into the grotto. It was a dark, smoky grotto, and in the middle of it there was a big frying-pan full of hot oil, which smelled like a snuffed-out candle, and nearly took one's breath away.

" Now, let's see what sort of fish we've caught ! " said the green fisherman, and, putting one of his big, misshapen hands, which looked like shovels, into the net, he drew out a handful of mullet.

" These mullet will be good ! " he said, looking at them, and smelling them contentedly ; then he threw them into a tub without any water in it.

He repeated this operation many times; and as he drew out the fish his mouth began to water, and he jumped for joy, saying :

" These haddock will be good ! "

" These whiting will be exquisite ! "

" These sole will be delicious ! "

" These sea spiders will be excellent ! "

" These anchovies will be fine, head an all ! "

As you may imagine the haddock, the whiting, the sole, the sea spiders, and the anchovies all went together into the tub, to keep the mullet company.

The last to come out of the net was Pinocchio.

When the fisherman pulled him out, he opened his green eyes wide in astonishment, and cried, almost in a fright :

" What sort of fish is this? I have never eaten a fish like this ! "

After turning him over and over, and examining him carefully, he finished by saying :

" I see : this must be a sea crab."

" What do you mean by calling me a crab ? This is a nice

way to treat me ! Let me tell you, for your information, that I am a marionette ! ''

" A marionette ? " said the fisherman. " To tell the truth, a marionette fish is a new one for me. All the better ! I shall eat you with the greatest pleasure ! "

" Eat me ? Can't you understand that I am not a fish ? Don't you see that I can talk and reason as you do ? "

" That's very true," replied the fisherman, " and since I see that you are a fish that can speak and reason like me, I will treat you with great consideration."

" And what may that mean ? "

" As a token of friendship and particular esteem, I will let you decide how you shall be cooked. Would you like to be fried in oil, or would you prefer to be cooked in the stewpan with tomato sauce ? "

" To tell the truth," replied Pinocchio, " if I must choose, I would prefer to be set free, so that I can go home."

" You're joking ! Do you think that I will lose this chance to taste such a rare fish ? It doesn't happen every day that one catches a marionette fish. Leave it to me : I will fry you in the pan with all the other fish, and you will be quite content. To be fried in company is always a consolation."

On hearing this, the unhappy Pinocchio cried and screamed, and begged for mercy, sobbing : " How much better it would have been if I had gone to school ! Oh ! Oh ! Oh ! " And because he squirmed like an eel, and put forth all his strength trying to escape from his claws, the green fisherman took a big bulrush, and after binding him hand and foot like a sausage, he threw him into the tub with the others.

Then he got a wooden keg full of flour, and began to roll all the fish in it; and as fast as he had floured them well he threw them into the frying-pan.

The first to dance in the boiling oil were the poor haddock : then came the spider crabs, the whiting, the sole, and the anchovies ; and then it was Pinocchio's turn, who, when he saw himself so near death, and such a terrible death, trembled so much, and was so dreadfully afraid that he could no longer find breath to beg for mercy.

The poor boy could only implore with his eyes ; but the green fisherman, without even looking at him, rolled him over five or six times in the flour, covering him so completely that he looked like a plaster marionette.

Then he took him by the head and . . .

CHAPTER TWENTY-NINE

Pinocchio Returns to the Fairy's House: she Promises him that the Next Day he will no Longer be a Marionette, but a Real Boy: Grand Breakfast of Coffee and Cream to Celebrate the Coming Event

JUST as the fisherman was about to drop Pinocchio into the frying-pan, a large dog came into the grotto, drawn there by the delicious, penetrating odour of the frying fish.

" Get out ! " cried the fisherman, menacing him, and still holding the floury marionette in his hand.

But the poor dog was almost starved. He howled, and wagged his tail as if to say :

" Just give me one mouthful, and I'll go away."

" Get out, I tell you ! " repeated the fisherman, drawing back his foot to kick him.

But the dog was so hungry that he was determined not to be kicked out, and he growled at the fisherman, showing his sharp teeth.

Just then a faint little voice was heard saying :

" Save me, Alidoro, if you don't save me I shall be fried ! "

The dog instantly recognised Pinocchio's voice, and he was amazed to see that it came from that floury bundle that the fisherman held in his hand.

What did he do then ? He jumped high in the air, seized the bundle, and holding it carefully between his teeth ran out of the grotto and away like the wind.

The fisherman was frightfully angry to see the fish that he was so eager to taste snatched away from him, and he ran after the dog ; but he had run only a little way when he had a violent fit of coughing, and had to go back home.

When Alidoro came to the path that led to the village, he stopped and put Pinocchio down gently on the ground.

" How can I ever thank you ? " said the marionette.

" You need not thank me," replied the dog ; " you saved my life, and one good turn deserves another. You know we must all help each other in this world."

" How did you happen to come to the grotto ? "

" I was lying on the beach more dead than alive, when the wind brought me the odour of frying fish. That gave me an appetite, and I followed the smell of the fish. If I had been a moment later ! . . ."

" Don't speak of it ! " exclaimed Pinocchio, who was still trembling with fear. " Don't speak of it ! If you had come a moment later, I should be, at this very instant, fried, and eaten, and digested. Br-r-r-r ! It makes me shiver to think of it ! "

Alidoro laughed and held out his right paw to the marionette, who grasped it and pressed it hard, as a sign of friendship, and then they parted.

The dog went home ; but when Pinocchio was alone he went to a little cabin nearby where an old man was sunning himself at the door, and said :

" Tell me, kind sir, do you know anything about a poor boy named Eugene who was wounded on the head ? "

" Some fishermen brought him here to this cabin, but now . . ."

" Now he is dead ! " Pinocchio interrupted sadly.

" No, he is alive, and has gone back home."

" Truly ? Truly ? " cried the marionette, jumping for joy. " So then his wound wasn't serious ? "

" It might have been serious ; it might even have killed him," replied the old man, " for they threw a large bound book at his head."

" Who threw it ? "

" One of his schoolmates, a certain Pinocchio."

" Who is this Pinocchio ? " inquired the marionette, as if he had never heard of him.

" They say he's a very bad boy, a vagabond, and a perfect scallywag."

" Slanders! All slanders ! "

" Do you know this Pinocchio ? "

"I know him by sight," replied the little marionette.

"And what do you think of him?" asked the old man.

"I think he is a very good boy who loves to study, who is obedient, and who loves his father and his family."

While the marionette was telling all these bold-faced lies, he happened to touch his nose, and seeing that it had grown several inches, he cried in a fright:

"No, kind sir, don't believe what I have told you! I know Pinocchio very well, and I assure you that he really is a very bad boy. He is a laggard, and disobedient, and instead of going to school he spends his time with evil companions."

As soon as he had said this, his nose grew shorter, and became as it was at first.

"Why are you so white?" asked the old man suddenly.

"I'll tell you. Without noticing it I rubbed against a wall that had just been whitewashed," replied the marionette, for he was ashamed to confess that he had been rolled in flour like a fish, in order to be fried.

"But what has become of your jacket, and your trousers, and your cap? What have you done with them?"

"I met thieves, and they robbed me of my clothes. Tell me, kind sir, do you happen to have some old clothes you could give me, so that I can go home?"

"My child, I have nothing but a little bag in which I keep beans; if you want that, take it: there it is."

Pinocchio didn't think twice, but he took the little bean bag, which was empty, and after cutting a hole in the bottom with scissors, and one on each side for his arms, he put it on like a little shirt. And in that excuse for clothes he started for home.

But as he went along he began to feel very uneasy. He took one step forward, and then one backwards, as he said to himself:

"How can I show myself to that kind Fairy? What will she say when she sees me? Will she forgive this second offence? I don't believe she will; oh, I'm sure she will not. And it will serve me right, for I am a bad boy, always promising to do better, and never keeping my word."

He arrived in the village after dark, and because it was a stormy night, and the rain was coming down in bucketfuls, he went straight to the Fairy's house, resolved to knock at the door and ask for shelter.

But when he came to the door he was afraid to knock, and ran back a little way; he came up to the door a second time, but he could not bring himself to knock; a third time, it was just the same: the fourth time he took hold of the iron knocker and let it fall very lightly, trembling as he did so.

He waited and waited, and at last, after half an hour, a window on the top floor was opened (the house had four floors) and a big snail with a tiny light on her head looked out, and said:

" Who is it, at this hour ? "

" Is the Fairy at home ? " asked Pinocchio.

" The Fairy is asleep and does not want to be disturbed ! But who are you ? "

" I am I."

" I ? Who is I ? "

" Pinocchio."

" Who is Pinocchio ? "

" The marionette who lives with the Fairy."

" Ah ! I see," said the Snail; " wait for me. I will come down at once and open the door."

" Hurry, for pity's sake, I am dying of cold ! "

" My son, I am a Snail, and Snails are never in a hurry."

An hour passed, two hours, and the door was not opened; so Pinocchio, who was shaking with cold and fright and dampness, plucked up his courage and knocked once more, a little louder.

At this a window opened on the third floor, and the same Snail looked out.

" Kind Snail," cried Pinocchio from the street, " I have been waiting two hours ! And two hours in this horrid weather are longer than two years. Hurry up, for mercy's sake ! "

" My son," said that sluggish, peaceful Snail, " my son, I am a Snail, and Snails are never in a hurry."

And the window on the third floor was closed.

Not long after the village clock struck midnight; then one o'clock, two o'clock, and the door was still closed.

Finally Pinocchio lost his patience. He seized the knocker in a rage, and was about to strike a blow that would shake the whole house, when suddenly the iron knocker turned into a live eel, slipped out of his hands, and disappeared in the rivulets of water that were running in the street.

"Oh, ho!" shouted Pinocchio, boiling over with rage, "if the knocker has run away, I will kick the door down!"

And drawing back, he let fly a furious kick against the door. He kicked so hard that half his foot went through the door, and when he tried to pull it back, it was impossible. His foot was stuck in the door as firmly as a nail that has been driven in and clinched.

Imagine poor Pinocchio now! He had to pass all the rest of the night with one foot on the ground, and the other in the door.

Finally, at daybreak, the door was opened. That obliging Snail had spent only nine hours coming down from the fourth story to the street door. She must have been all of a lather!

"What are you doing there, with your foot sticking in the door?" she inquired, laughing.

"It was an accident. Won't you please see, kind Snail, if you can free me from this torment?"

"My son, this is a case for a carpenter, and I have never been a carpenter."

"Beg the Fairy to help me."

"The Fairy is sleeping, and does not want to be disturbed."

"But what am I going to do all day, riveted to this door?"

"You can amuse yourself by counting the ants that crawl by."

"At least bring me something to eat, for I am faint with hunger."

"Immediately!" said the Snail.

In fact three hours and a half later Pinocchio saw her coming back with a tray on her head. There was bread, a roast chicken, and four ripe apricots.

"Here is the breakfast the Fairy sends you," said the Snail.

At the sight of all those good things the marionette was quite consoled. But how great was his disappointment, when he began to eat, to discover that the bread was plaster, the chicken was made of paper, and the four apricots of alabaster, coloured to look like the fruit.

He wanted to weep, to resign himself to despair, to throw away the tray and all that was on it; instead, whether because of his grief, or the great weakness he felt in his stomach, the fact is that he fainted away.

When he came to himself he was lying on a sofa, and the Fairy was bending over him.

"I will forgive you just once more," said the Fairy, "but woe betide you if you do wrong again."

Pinocchio promised and vowed that he would study, and always be good; and he kept his word all the rest of the year. He stood first in the examinations, and was called the best scholar in the school. His conduct in general was so satisfactory and praiseworthy, that the Fairy was greatly pleased, and said:

"To-morrow your desires shall finally be granted."

"Do you mean . . . ?"

"To-morrow you shall cease to be a wooden marionette, and become a real boy."

No one who did not see Pinocchio at the moment when he received this longed-for announcement can imagine his joy. All his friends and classmates were invited to the Fairy's house the next day, for a grand breakfast to celebrate the wonderful event. The Fairy prepared two hundred cups of coffee with cream, and four hundred rolls, buttered on both sides. The day promised to be a most happy and joyful one, but . . .

Most unfortunately, in the lives of marionettes there is always a *but* that spoils everything.

CHAPTER THIRTY

Pinocchio Listens to his Friend Lampwick, who is Going to Toyland

As was to be expected, Pinocchio asked the Fairy's permission to go around the village and invite his friends for the next day. The Fairy said :

" Yes, indeed, go and invite all your friends for breakfast, but remember to come home before dark. Do you understand ? "

" I promise to be back in an hour," said the marionette.

" Be careful, Pinocchio ; it's very easy for children to promise, but not so easy for them to keep their promises."

" But I am not like other children ; when I say a thing, I do it."

" We shall see. If you do disobey me, the worse for you."

" Why ? "

" Because children who do not listen to those who are wiser than they are always come to grief."

" And I have proved it ! " said Pinocchio ; " but I shall never be naughty again."

" We shall see if that is true."

The marionette said no more, but kissed the kind Fairy, who was a sort of mother to him, and ran out of the house singing and dancing.

In less than an hour all his friends had been invited. Some of them accepted immediately with great pleasure ; others, on principle waited to be urged ; but when they learned that the rolls which were to be dipped in the coffee and cream would be buttered on both sides, they all said : " Yes, we'll come too, just to please you."

Now I must tell you that Pinocchio had among his schoolmates one of whom he was especially fond. His name was Romeo, but everybody called him by his nickname of " Lampwick," because he was so thin, and long, and flabby just like a new lampwick.

Lampwick was the laziest and most mischievous boy in the school, but Pinocchio was very fond of him. In fact, he went to his home first of all, but he was not there. He went back again, but no Lampwick; a third time, but in vain.

Wherever could he be? He searched high and low, and finally found him hiding under the porch of a farmer's house.

" What in the world are you doing there?" inquired Pinocchio, crawling under the porch.

" I'm waiting for midnight, when I'm going away."

" Where are you going?"

" Far, far away."

" I went to your house three times looking for you."

" What do you want of me?"

" Haven't you heard the great news? Don't you know of the good fortune that's coming to me?"

" What?"

" To-morrow I shall stop being a marionette, and become a boy like you, and like all the others."

" Much good may it do you!"

" And to-morrow morning I shall expect you at my house for breakfast."

" But didn't I tell you that I am going away to-night?"

" At what time?"

" At midnight."

" Where are you going?"

" I'm going to live in a place—the most beautiful place in the world—a perfect paradise!"

" What is the name of it?"

" It's called Toyland. Why don't you come too?"

" I? No, indeed!"

" You're making a mistake, Pinocchio! Believe me, if you don't come you will regret it. Where could you find a place better suited to us boys? There's no school there, and no masters, and no books. In that blessed place no one ever studies. There's no school on Saturday; and every week is composed of six Saturdays, and one Sunday. Just imagine! The autumn holidays begin in January, and last until the thirty-first of December. Now that's a place where I would really like to live! That's how all civilised countries should be!"

" But how do they pass the time in Toyland?"

" They play and amuse themselves from morning till night. Then they go to bed, and begin over again in the morning. What do you think of that?"

" Ummm!" said Pinocchio, and he wagged his head as if to say: " That sort of life would suit me too."

" Now then, will you come with me? Yes, or no, make up your mind!"

" No, no, no, and no. I have promised the kind Fairy that I would be a good boy and, I must keep my promise. In fact, I see it's nearly sunset, so I must leave you and hurry away. Good-bye, and a pleasant journey."

" Where are you going in such a hurry?"

" I'm going home. The kind Fairy wants me to come home before dark."

" Wait a little bit."

" I shall be too late."

" Just two minutes."

" And if the Fairy should scold me?"

" Let her scold. When she's done scolding, she'll stop," said that scamp of a Lampwick.

" How are you going? Alone, or is someone going with you?"

" Alone? There will be more than a hundred of us!"

" Are you going on foot?"

" A stagecoach is coming at midnight to take us to that glorious country."

" What wouldn't I give if it were midnight now!"

" And why?"

" So that I could see you all go off together."

" Stay a little longer, and you can see us."

" No, no, I must go home."

"Just wait only two more minutes." Lampwick pleaded.

"I have waited too long, now. The Fairy will be worrying about me."

"Poor Fairy! Is she afraid the bats will eat you?"

"And so," continued Pinocchio, "are you perfectly certain there are no schools in that country?"

"Not a sign of one!"

"And no masters?"

"Not one."

"And no one ever has to study?"

"Never, never, never!"

"What a wonderful country!" sighed Pinocchio. His mouth watered just to think of it. "What a wonderful country! Of course I've never been there, but I can imagine what it must be like."

"Why don't you come too?"

"It's useless to tempt me. I have promised my kind Fairy that I would be a sensible boy, and I don't propose to break my word."

"Well, good-bye then, and give my love to all the grammar schools, and to all the high schools, too, if you meet them on the way."

"Good-bye, Lampwick; a pleasant journey to you. Have a fine time, and remember your friends once in a while."

Saying this the marionette took a few steps as if to leave him; then stopped and turning to his friend he inquired:

"Are you perfectly certain that all the weeks are composed of six Saturdays and one Sunday in that country?"

"Absolutely."

"Are you perfectly certain that holidays begin on the first of January, and last until the thirty-first of December?"

"Perfectly certain."

"What a wonderful country!" said Pinocchio again, smacking his lips in a transport of delight.

Then, summoning all his resolution, he added hastily:

"Well, good-bye for the last time, and a good journey to you!"

" Good-bye for the last time to you, Pinocchio."

" How long before you leave ? "

" About two hours."

" Too bad ! If it were only one hour, I might, perhaps, wait to see you off."

" And the Fairy ? "

" I have waited so long already, that an hour more or less wouldn't matter."

" Poor Pinocchio ! And what if the Fairy should scold you ? "

" Never mind ! I would let her scold ; when she's done scolding she'll stop."

By this time it was very dark. Suddenly, far away, they saw a little light moving, and heard bells tinkling, and the tooting of a tiny horn, very faint and low, like the hum of a bee.

" There it is ! " exclaimed Lampwick, jumping to his feet.

" What is it ? " said Pinocchio in a low tone.

" It's the stagecoach coming to get me. Do you want to go too ? Yes, or no ? "

" But is it actually true," demanded the marionette, " that children never have to study in that country ? "

" Never, never, never ! "

" What a wonderful country ! What a wonderful country ! What a wonderful country ! "

CHAPTER THIRTY-ONE

*Instead of Becoming a Real Boy, Pinocchio Steals Away to
Toyland where he Spends Five Months of Paradise*

AT last the stagecoach arrived; and it drove up without
making the least noise, for the wheels were wound with rags
and tow.

It was drawn by twelve pairs of donkeys, all of the same
size, but of different colours.

Some were grey, some white, some spotted, and some were
yellow and blue in broad stripes.

But the strangest thing about them was that these twelve
pairs, or twenty-four donkeys, instead of being shod like
most other animals, wore men's boots of white calfskin.

And the driver?

Imagine a little man broader than he is long, soft and oily
as a butterball, with a little face like a red apple, a little mouth
that is always laughing, and a soft, caressing voice like that of a
cat that is mewing for cream.

All the boys fell in love with him as soon as they saw him;
and they all scrambled to get in first, and go with him to that
delightful country which is known on the map by the enticing
name of Toyland.

Indeed the stagecoach was already full of boys between
eight and twelve years of age, huddled together like so many
sardines. They were so crowded and uncomfortable that they
could hardly breathe, but no one said *ouch!* no one complained.
The consolation of knowing that in a few hours they would
be in a country where there were no books, or schools, or
masters, made them feel resigned to anything. They were so
happy that they were neither uncomfortable, nor weary, nor
hungry, nor thirsty, nor sleepy.

As soon as the stagecoach stopped, the little man turned to

Lampwick, and with a thousand bows and grimaces, said with the sweetest of smiles :

" Tell me, my fine boy, would you like to go to that happy country ? "

" Certainly, I want to go."

" But you see, my dear, there is no more room, the coach is full."

" Never mind," replied Lampwick, " if there's no more room inside, I can ride on the swingle-tree."

And he jumped up astride of the swingle-tree.

" And you, my love," said the little man, looking admiringly at Pinocchio, " what are you going to do ? Are you coming with us, or staying behind ? "

" I remain here," replied Pinocchio, " I am going home. I want to study and be a good scholar, like all well-brought-up boys."

" Much good may it do you ! "

" Pinocchio," cried Lampwick, " listen to me : come with us, we will be so happy."

" No, no, no ! "

" Come away with us, we will all be so happy ! " cried a few voices inside the stagecoach.

" Come with us, we will all be so happy," shouted a hundred voices together.

" If I should come with you, what would my good Fairy say ? "

" Don't worry yourself about that. Only remember that we are going to a country where we shall do nothing but frolic from morning till night."

Pinocchio did not reply : he only sighed ; he sighed a second time ; a third. At last he said :

" Make a little room for me : I will come too."

" Everything is full," replied the little man, " but to show you how glad I am that you are coming with me, I will give you my place."

" What will you do ? "

" I will walk."

"No, really, I can't let you do that. I would rather ride on one of the donkeys!" cried Pinocchio.

So saying he went up to the right wheeler, and made as if to jump on his back, but the beast whirled and kicked him in the stomach, sending him flying with his legs in the air.

Imagine, if you can, how all those impertinent boys nearly burst themselves laughing.

But the little man did not laugh. He just went up to that donkey, and pretending to give him a kiss, he bit off half of his right ear.

While he was doing this, Pinocchio, who was very angry at the treatment he had received, jumped up from the ground, and with one leap was on the donkey's back. It was such a splendid jump that all the boys stopped laughing, and shouted, "Hurray for Pinocchio!" and they clapped their hands as if they would never stop.

But all of a sudden the donkey kicked so high with both his hind legs that he threw the poor marionette off on to a pile of stones.

The boys began to laugh at him again; but the little man, instead of laughing, went to the other side of that fractious animal, and bit half of his left ear clean off. Then he said to the marionette:

"Now get on his back, and don't be afraid. That donkey is as obstinate as a mule; but I've put a flea in his ear, and I think he'll behave himself now."

Pinocchio mounted again, and the stagecoach began to move; but while the donkeys galloped along, and the coach rolled over the paving-stones, he thought he heard a voice which was so low that he could barely make out the words, saying:

"You poor simpleton! You are determined to do as you please, but you will be sorry for it!"

Pinocchio was frightened, and looked around him to see where these words came from, but there was nothing to be seen. The donkeys galloped along, the stagecoach rolled over the stones, and the boys inside slept. Lampwick snored like a trooper, and the little man sang through his teeth:

" Everyone sleeps all through the night,
While I, never sleep . . ."

They had gone only a little way farther when Pinocchio heard the low voice again saying :

" Remember this, you little blockhead, boys who will not study, and who turn their backs on their school, and their books, and their masters, always come to a bad end. I have tried it, and I know what I am talking about. The day will come when you will weep as I do now, but then it will be too late ! "

When he heard these whispered words, the marionette was more frightened than ever. He jumped down from the donkey's back, and took him by the bridle.

Imagine his surprise when he saw that the donkey was crying, and crying just like a child !

" Hallo, little man," Pinocchio called to the driver, " do you know what's happening ? This donkey is crying."

" Let him cry ! He can laugh on the thirty-first of June."

" Did you teach him to speak ? "

" No, he taught himself to mumble a few words ; he was in a company of trained dogs for three years."

" Poor beast ! "

" Come, come," said the little man, " don't waste time watching a donkey cry. Get on his back again, and let us go. The night is chilly, and the way is long."

Pinocchio did as he was told, without another word. The stagecoach rolled along once more, and at daybreak the next morning they reached Toyland, safe and sound.

Toyland was like no other country in the world. The entire population consisted of children. The eldest were fourteen, and the youngest barely eight years old. The clamour and shouting and hullabaloo in the streets were enough to drive one crazy.

There were swarms of children everywhere. Some were playing skittles; others were playing quoits, or rounders; some were riding bicycles or wooden horses ; others were playing blind-man's buff, or tig; some of them, dressed as clowns, were eating burning tow; some were playing comedies, or singing, or turning somersaults in the air ; others were walking on their hands, while still others were rolling hoops, or, dressed like generals, were marching along with paper helmets on their heads, and squadrons of toy soldiers. They were hallooing and laughing, and shouting ; some were clapping their hands ; some were whistling ; some were cackling like a hen that has laid an egg ; in short, there was such a chattering, such a pandemonium, such a wild tumult, that it would have made you deaf, unless you had put cotton wool in your ears. There were little theatres in every open space which were crowded all the day long ; and on all the walls of the houses refined remarks like the following had been scrawled with coal : " Hurrah for Toiland ! " (instead of Toyland). " We want no more scools ! " (instead of schools). " Down with Arit Metick ! " (instead of arithmetic) ; and many more fine sayings like these.

As soon as they set foot inside the city, Lampwick, and all the other boys who had come with the little man, hurried to join these children, and in a few minutes, as you may well suppose, they had made friends with them all. Who could be more happy and contented than they were ?

In the midst of continual amusement and all sorts of pastimes, the hours and days and weeks passed like lightning.

" Oh, what a glorious life ! " exclaimed Pinocchio, every time he happened to run across Lampwick.

" Do you see now that I was right ? " replied Lampwick. " And to think that you didn't want to come ! To think that you were going to go back home to your Fairy, and waste your time in study ! If you are free to-day from bothersome books and schools, you owe it to me, to my advice, to my anxiety for your welfare. Isn't that so ? It's only a true friend who would do you such a great kindness."

" Yes, that's so, Lampwick ! If I am to-day a perfectly contented boy it's all owing to you. And do you know what the Master used to say to me about you ? He always said : ' Don't have anything to do with that good-for-nothing

Lampwick ; he is a bad boy, and he will get you into trouble.' "

" Poor old Master ! " replied the other, shaking his head. " I know only too well that he didn't like me, and enjoyed speaking ill of me ; but I am generous, and I forgive him ! "

" You noble boy ! " said Pinocchio, embracing his friend affectionately, and kissing him on the bridge of his nose.

Five months had passed away in this paradise of playthings and amusements which occupied the whole of the day, without ever looking a book in the face, or seeing so much as the outside of a school, when Pinocchio, on waking up one morning, had a most unpleasant surprise, and quite lost his good spirits.

CHAPTER THIRTY-TWO

Pinocchio Grows Donkey's Ears and then Becomes a Real Donkey and Begins to Bray

AND what was this surprise?

I will tell you, my dear readers: The surprise was that Pinocchio when he woke up began, naturally, to scratch his head; and while he was doing this he . . .

Can you guess what he noticed?

He noticed, to his great astonishment, that his ears had grown several inches longer.

You know, marionettes, from their birth, have very, very small ears ; so small that they are not visible to the naked eye. You can imagine, therefore, how startled he was when he became aware that his ears had grown so long during the night that they resembled two sweeping brushes.

He hurried in search of a mirror in order to see himself, but he could not find one : so he filled the hand-basin with water and looking into it saw, what he would never in the world have wanted to see, he saw himself decorated with a magnificent pair of asses' ears.

I will leave you to imagine poor Pinocchio's sorrow, and shame and despair.

He began to cry, and scream, and beat his head against the wall, but the more he wept, the longer his ears grew, and they became hairy at the top.

A pretty little squirrel that lived on the floor above him heard his piercing cries, and came down to see what the matter was ; and seeing the marionette in such a state, she inquired anxiously :

" What is the matter, my dear neighbour ? "

" I am sick. Oh, Squirrel, I am very sick, and of such a frightful disease. Do you know how to count one's pulse ? "

" Yes, I believe so."

" Then, Squirrel, will you please see if I have a fever ? "

The Squirrel put her right front paw on Pinocchio's wrist, and then said with a sigh :

" My friend, I am sorry, but I must give you bad news."

" What is it ? "

" You have a raging fever."

" What kind of fever is it ? "

" Donkey fever."

" I never heard of any such fever ! " retorted the marionette, although he knew only too well what she meant.

" Then I will tell you about it," replied the Squirrel, " for you should know that in two or three hours you will no longer be a marionette, or a boy . . ."

" What will I be ? "

" In two or three hours you will be a perfect donkey, like those that draw carts, and carry cabbages and herbs to market."

" Oh ! Poor me ! Poor me ! " cried Pinocchio, seizing his ears with both hands, and twitching and jerking them angrily, as if they belonged to someone else.

" My dear," said the Squirrel by way of consolation, " what would you have ? It is your destiny. For it is written in the decrees of Providence that all those lazy children who can't endure books, and schools, and masters, and who pass their time with toys and games, and amusements, must finish, sooner or later, by becoming so many little donkeys."

" Is that really true ? " sobbed the marionette.

" It's only too true ! It's useless to weep now. You should have thought of that before it was too late."

" But it's not my fault : believe me, little Squirrel, it's all Lampwick's fault ! "

" Who is this Lampwick ? "

" One of my schoolmates. I wanted to go home ; I wanted to be obedient ; I wanted to study and do myself credit . . . but Lampwick said : ' Why do you bother about studying ? Why in the world do you want to go to school ? Instead, come with me to Toyland : there we will never study any more ; we will play from morning to night, and always be happy ! ' "

"Why did you take the advice of that false friend? Of that bad companion?"

"Because . . . because, dear little Squirrel, I am a heartless marionette, without any sense. Oh, if I had had the least bit of heart, I never should have abandoned that kind Fairy who loved me like a mother, and who had done so much for me! . . . and at this hour I should no longer be a marionette, but a fine boy, like the others! Oh! If I meet Lampwick, he'd better look out for himself! I'll fix him!"

He started to go out of the room, but in the doorway he remembered that he had asses' ears, and he was ashamed to be seen. So then what did he do? He took a large cotton cap, and pulled it down over his head, right down to his nose.

Then he went out, and began to look for Lampwick. He searched the streets, the squares, the theatres, everywhere, but he could not find him. He inquired of everyone he met, but no one had seen him.

At last he went to his house and knocked at the door.

"Who is it?" said Lampwick, who was inside.

"Pinocchio," said the marionette.

"Wait a minute, and I'll let you in."

After half an hour the door was opened. Imagine Pinocchio's surprise, when he went in, to find that his friend Lampwick wore a great cotton cap that came down over the end of his nose.

At that sight Pinocchio was somewhat consoled, and he said to himself:

"Perhaps he is sick the same as I am. Can it be that he, too, has the donkey fever?"

But he pretended not to notice anything, and said with a smile:

"How are you, my dear Lampwick?"

"Very well, indeed, like a mouse in a Parmesan cheese."

"Do you really mean it?"

"And why should I tell you a lie?"

"Pardon me, my friend, but why then do you wear that cap that covers your ears?"

" The doctor prescribed it, because I have hurt my knee. And you, dear marionette, why do you wear that cap that comes down over your nose ? "

" The doctor prescribed it, because I bruised my shin."

" Oh ! Poor Pinocchio ! "

" Oh ! Poor Lampwick ! "

A long silence followed, during which the two friends gazed at each other ironically.

At last the marionette said in a sweet, insinuating voice :

" Just to satisfy my curiosity, dear Lampwick, won't you tell me if you ever had any disease in your ears ? "

" Never ! And you ? "

" Never ! Although I have had the earache in one ear this morning."

" Yes, so have I."

" You, too ? Which ear is it that aches ? "

" Both of them. And you ? "

" Both of them. Do you suppose it's the same disease ? "

" I'm afraid it is."

" Will you do me a favour, Lampwick ? "

" Yes, indeed, with all my heart."

" Will you let me see your ears ? "

" Why not ? But first I want to see yours, dear Pinocchio."

" No, you first."

" No, my dear, you first, and then I'll show mine."

" Well," said the marionette, " let us make a bargain, like good friends."

" Let us hear the bargain."

" We'll take off our caps at the same time. Agreed ? "

" Agreed."

" Now, ready ! "

And Pinocchio began to count in a loud voice :

" One ! Two ! Three ! "

At " Three ! " they took off their caps, and threw them in the air.

And then something unbelievable happened. When Pinocchio and Lampwick saw that the same misfortune had befallen them both, instead of feeling ashamed and sorry, they began to wag their long ears and laugh at each other.

They laughed and laughed, until they had to hold their sides : but suddenly Lampwick became silent ; he staggered and turned pale as he exclaimed :

" Help, help, Pinocchio ! "

" What is the matter ? "

" Alas ! I can't stand up straight."

" Neither can I," cried Pinocchio, stumbling and weeping.

While they were speaking they went down on all fours, and began to run around the room on their hands and feet. As they ran their arms became legs, their faces grew longer, and became muzzles, and their backs were covered with light grey hair, spotted with black.

But the most terrible moment for those two miserable boys— the most humiliating moment—was when they felt their tails sprouting. Overcome then by shame and sorrow, they began to weep and lament over their unhappy fate.

Oh, if they had only been silent ! Instead of groans and lamentations, they brayed like donkeys. Yes, both together, in chorus, they brayed loud and clear : " Hee-haw ! Hee-haw ! Hee-haw ! "

Meanwhile there was a knock at the door, and a voice cried :

" Open the door ! I am the little man, the driver of the stagecoach which brought you here. Open quickly, or it will be the worse for you ! "

CHAPTER THIRTY-THREE

Having Become a Real Donkey, Pinocchio is Sold to the Ring-master of a Show who Teaches him to Dance and Jump through a Hoop : but he is Lamed One Evening and then is Bought by a Man who Wishes to Make a Drum out of his Skin

SEEING that they did not open the door, the little man kicked it open and said, with his usual chuckle :

" Hurrah for you ! You brayed very well ; I recognised you at once. And now here I am."

Hearing these words the two donkeys stood very still, with their heads hanging down, and their tails between their legs.

At first the little man stroked and caressed and patted them ; then drawing forth a curry comb, he curried them well. When they shone so that you could see your face in them, he bridled them, and took them to market, hoping to sell them for a round sum. In fact, buyers were not lacking.

Lampwick was bought by a farmer whose donkey had died the day before : and Pinocchio was sold to the Ringmaster of a company of clowns and rope-walkers, who intended to teach him to jump and dance with the other animals belonging to the company.

Do you understand now, my readers, the fine business which the little man carried on ? This cruel little monster, who seemed all milk and honey, went about the world with his coach from time to time. By means of promises and caresses he collected all the children who did not like their books, and did not want to go to school, and after packing them into his coach he carried them off to Toyland, so that they could spend all their time playing and amusing themselves. When these poor children, by reason of always playing and never studying, became so many donkeys, he was very happy, and he took them to market and sold them. In a few years, by this means, he had become a millionaire.

I do not know what happened to Lampwick, but I know that Pinocchio, from the beginning, led a life of drudgery and abuse.

When he was led into the stable his new master filled his manger with straw, but Pinocchio spat it out after he had tasted it.

Then his master, grumbling, filled the manger with hay, but Pinocchio did not like that either.

" Ah ! You don't even like hay ? " cried his master angrily. " Leave it to me, my fine donkey, if you are going to be particular, I know how to cure you ! "

And as a beginning he struck his legs with his whip.

The pain made Pinocchio cry, and bray : " Hee-haw ! I can't digest straw ! "

" Then eat hay," replied his master, who understood donkey dialect perfectly.

" Hee-haw ! Hay gives me the stomach-ache ! "

" Do you think that I am going to feed a donkey like you on chicken breasts and capon cutlets ? " said his master still more angrily, and he gave him another cut with the whip.

After this second slash Pinocchio thought it would be wiser to keep quiet, and he said no more. The stable door was shut, and Pinocchio was left alone. It was so long since he had eaten anything that hunger made him yawn ; and as he yawned he opened a great mouth as large as an oven.

At last, since there was nothing else in his manger, he resigned himself to eat a little hay, and after chewing it a long time, he shut his eyes and swallowed it.

" This hay isn't bad," he said to himself, " but how much better it would have been if I had kept on with my studies ! By this time, instead of hay, I might be eating the crusty end of a fresh loaf, with a fine slice of sausage ! Patience ! "

As soon as he was awake in the morning, he looked for a little more hay ; but he found none, for he had eaten it all during the night.

Then he tried a mouthful of chopped straw, but as he chewed away at it he thought what a difference there was between the taste of chopped straw, and rice, as it is served in Milan, or macaroni, as they cook it in Naples.

"Patience!" he said again, as he continued to chew. "At least my misfortune may serve as a lesson to disobedient children who hate to study. Patience! Patience!"

"Patience, my hat!" shouted his master, who came into the stable at that moment. "Do you imagine, my fine donkey, that I bought you just to feed you? I bought you to work, and help me make money. Come on, now, and do your best! Come into the Circus, and I'll teach you to jump through a hoop and break a paper ring with your head, and to waltz and polka on your hind legs."

So poor Pinocchio, for love or by force, had to learn all these fine tricks; but it took him three months, with many sharp cuts of the whip.

At last the day came when his master announced a really wonderful show. Gaily-coloured posters were pasted up at all the street corners, which read thus:

GRAND GALA SPECTACLE

This evening
THE USUAL DARING LEAPS
AND ASTOUNDING FEATS
BY ALL THE ARTISTES
And by all the horses of the company
EXTRA!
*There will appear for the first time
the famous*
LITTLE DONKEY PINOCCHIO
called
THE STAR OF THE DANCE
The theatre will be brilliantly illuminated

You may take my word for it, that the theatre was full an hour before the performance.

Not another seat could have been purchased even for its weight in gold. All the seats around the ring were filled with girls and boys who were wild to see the famous donkey Pinocchio dancing.

When the first part of the show was over, the Ringmaster came before the audience. He wore a black coat, white tights, and boots that reached above his knees. After making a very low bow, he delivered the following ridiculous speech :

" Honourable public, ladies and gentleman !

" The humble undersigned, who is stopping in your city for a time, wishes to have the honour and pleasure of presenting to this intelligent and noble audience a celebrated little donkey, who has had the honour of dancing before the Emperors of all the principal courts of Europe.

" I thank you for your attention, and beg that you will assist us by your inspiring presence, and excuse our short-comings."

This discourse was received with much laughter and applause; but the applause was redoubled and became a veritable tempest at the appearance of the Little Donkey Pinocchio in the middle of the ring. He was magnificently dressed up ! He had a new bridle of shiny leather, with buckles and studs of brass, and a white camellia behind each ear. His mane was divided into tiny curls, each one decorated with a white silk tassel ; a broad band of gold and silver ran round his body, and his tail was braided with red and blue velvet ribbons. In short, he was a darling little donkey.

In presenting him to the public the manager added these words :

" Honourable audience ! I am not here to deceive you as to the immense difficulties I had to overcome in order to capture and subjugate this mammal as he was feeding, wild and free, from mountain to mountain in the plains of the torrid zone. Observe, I implore you, the ferocity which gleams in his eyes, so that when every other means of domesticating him failed,

I was forced to resort to the lash. But in spite of all my kindness, which should have aroused his love for me, he has grown fiercer day by day. However, following the system of Galles, I found in his cranium a bump, which the Faculty of Medicine in Paris declare to be the regenerator of the hair and of the Pyrrhic dance. On account of this, I have taught him to dance, and also to jump through a hoop, and casks lined with paper. Admire him, and judge him! But before I take my leave of you, permit me to invite you to the daily spectacle to-morrow evening. But if bad weather threatens to rain, then the show, instead of to-morrow evening, will be set back to to-morrow morning, at eleven o'clock in the afternoon."

Here the Ringmaster made another low bow, and then, turning to Pinocchio, he exclaimed :

" Come, Pinocchio, before beginning your performance, salute this honourable audience : the ladies and the gentleman, and the children ! "

Pinocchio obediently bent his forelegs, and remained kneeling until the Ringmaster cracked his whip and cried :

" Walk ! "

Then the little donkey got up and went round the ring, walking all the time.

After a bit the Ringmaster cried :

" Trot !" Pinocchio obeyed the command, and began to trot.

" Gallop ! "—and Pinocchio broke into a gallop.

" Run ! "—and Pinocchio ran with all his might. Suddenly the Ringmaster raised his arm in the air and fired off a pistol.

At that the donkey pretended to be wounded, and fell down in the ring as if he were dead.

He rose up amid shouts of applause and a clapping of hands that could have been heard for a mile away. Naturally he lifted his head to look up at the people, and there he saw, in one of the boxes, a lovely lady wearing a heavy gold chain round her neck, from which hung a medallion. On the medallion was the portrait of a marionette.

" That is my portrait ! . . . That lady is the Fairy ! " said

Pinocchio to himself, recognising her immediately; and he was so overcome with joy that he tried to cry out:

" Oh, my dear Fairy! Oh, my dear Fairy ! "

But instead of these words there issued forth from his throat a " Hee-haw ! " so long and loud that all the spectators laughed, and especially all the children who were present.

Then the Ringmaster, in order to teach him that it was not good manners to bray like that before the public, struck him lightly on the nose with his whip handle.

The poor little donkey put out his long tongue, and licked his nose at least five minutes, to comfort himself for the pain he felt.

But what was his despair when, turning to look at the box a second time, he saw that it was empty—the Fairy had disappeared !

He thought he was going to die; his eyes filled with tears and he began to weep bitterly. However, no one noticed it, least of all the Ringmaster, who cracked his whip and cried :

" Bravo, Pinocchio ! Now show these ladies and gentlemen how gracefully you can jump through the hoop."

Pinocchio tried two or three times : but every time he came up to the hoop he found it easier to run under it. At last he leapt through it, but his hind legs caught in the hoop, and he fell heavily to the ground.

When he got up he was lame, and could hardly walk back to the stable.

" Bring out Pinocchio ! We want the little donkey ! Bring out the little donkey ! " shouted the children, who were all very sorry for his accident.

But the little donkey was seen no more that evening.

When the veterinary surgeon—that is, the animal doctor—saw him the next morning, he declared that he would be lame for the rest of his life.

Then the Ringmaster said to his stable boy :

" What can I do with a lame donkey ? I would have to feed him for nothing. Take him to market and sell him."

As soon as they arrived at the market they found a purchaser who inquired :

" How much do you want for this lame donkey ? "

" Five pounds."

" I will give you fivepence. Don't imagine that he will be of any use to me. I am only buying him for his skin. I see he has a very hard skin, and I want to make a drum for the town band."

Only think how Pinocchio must have felt when he knew that he was destined to be a drum !

As soon as the fivepence was paid, his new owner led the little donkey to a rock by the sea, tied a stone around his neck, and a long rope to one leg. Then he suddenly gave him a push and he fell into the water.

Pinocchio, with that stone around his neck, went straight to the bottom ; and his owner, holding tight to the rope, sat down on the rock to wait until he was drowned, so that he could skin him.

CHAPTER THIRTY-FOUR

*Pinocchio, Thrown into the Sea and Eaten by the Fishes, Becomes
a Marionette again : but while he is Swimming for the Shore
he is Swallowed by a Terrible Shark*

WHEN the little donkey had been under water nearly an hour,
his new owner said to himself :

" That poor little lame donkey must surely be drowned
by this time ! Let us pull him up, and make a fine drum out
of his skin."

He began to pull in the rope, which he had tied to one of his
legs : he pulled, and pulled, and pulled, and at last there
appeared on the surface . . . can you guess ? Instead of a
dead donkey, there was a live marionette, wiggling like an eel.

When he saw that wooden marionette, the poor man thought
he must be dreaming. He was struck dumb, and stood
there with his mouth wide open and his eyes starting from
his head.

When he had come to himself a little he said, crying, and
stammering :

" Where . . . where is the little donkey I threw into the
water ? "

" I'm the little donkey ! " replied the marionette, laughing.

" You ! "

" Me ! "

" Ah, you rogue, don't try to play any tricks on me ! "

" Play tricks on you ? No, indeed, my dear master ; I am
perfectly serious."

" But how can it be that you, who were a little donkey a
few minutes ago, have now become a wooden marionette ? "

" It must be the effect of the sea water. It works that way
sometimes."

" Be careful, marionette, be careful ! Don't try to play any

137

jokes on me ! It will go hard with you if I lose my patience ! "

" Well, master, do you want to hear my true story ? If you will take this rope off my leg, I will tell it to you."

The good man was very curious to hear his story, so he quickly untied the rope on his leg. Then Pinocchio, free as a bird once more, began to speak as follows :

" You must know that I was once a wooden marionette, just as I am now ; and I was on the point of becoming a real boy, like so many others. But I didn't like to study, and I listened to evil companions, and so I ran away ; and one fine day I woke up to find myself a donkey with long ears, and a long tail. Oh, I was so ashamed of myself ! Oh, my dear master, may the good Saint Antonio keep you from ever feeling so ashamed ! I was taken to market with the other donkeys and sold to the Ringmaster of a circus. He made me learn to dance, and jump through a hoop, but one evening during the show I fell and lamed myself. The Ringmaster had no use for a lame donkey, and so he sent me back to the market, and you bought me."

" I know that only too well ! And I paid fivepence for you. And now who will give me back my five poor pennies ? "

" And why did you buy me ? To make a drum out of my skin ! A drum ! "

" That's only too true ! And now where will I find another skin ? "

" Don't despair, master, there are so many donkeys in this world ! "

" Well, you impertinent monkey, is that the end of your story ? "

" No," replied the marionette, " just two words more, and I am done. After having bought me, you brought me here to kill me ; and then because you were sorry for me, you preferred to tie a stone to my neck, and throw me into the sea. This delicate sentiment does you great honour, and I shall be eternally grateful to you. But this time, my dear master, you reckoned without the Fairy."

" And who is this Fairy ? "

" She is my mother, and she is like all other mothers who love their children dearly, and never lose sight of them, and help them in all their troubles, even when, because of their escapades and their naughty ways, they deserve to be left to themselves. So, as I was saying, as soon as the kind Fairy saw that I was in danger of drowning, she sent an immense shoal of fishes who thought that I was a dead donkey, and began to eat me. And what big bites they took ! I never would have believed that fishes could be more ravenous than boys ! Some ate my ears, others my muzzle, others my neck and mane, my hoofs, and even the skin off my back. And there was one of them that was so polite that he even condescended to eat my tail."

" From this day forward," said his horrified listener, " I vow never to eat another fish. It would be a pretty how-de-do to open a mullet, or a whiting, and find a donkey's tail inside it ! "

" I agree with you," said the marionette, laughing ; " as for that, you must know that when the fishes had eaten away all the donkey disguise that covered me from head to foot, they came, naturally, to the bones, or to be exact, to the wood, because, as you see, I am made of very hard wood. But after the first bite they saw that I was no longer meat for them, and disgusted by such indigestible food, they swam off in all directions, without even saying thank you. That is why when you pulled up the rope you found a live marionette, instead of a dead donkey."

" A fig for your story ! " cried the man in a rage. " I have paid fivepence for you, and I want my money back ! I know what I'll do ! I will take you back to the market and sell you for firewood."

" Sell me if you want to ; I wouldn't mind," said Pinocchio. But as he spoke he jumped as far as he could, and came down with a splash in the sea ; and as he swam gaily away he cried to the poor man who had bought him :

" Good-bye, master, when you want a skin to make a drum, remember me."

He continued to laugh as he swam farther away : after a little he turned again, and shouted louder than before :

" Good-bye master ! When you want a little nice dry firewood, remember me."

In the wink of an eye he was so far off that he could hardly be seen ; in fact, there was only a black dot on the surface of the water that now and then lifted an arm, or a leg, or jumped out of the water like a good-humoured dolphin.

Pinocchio was swimming without any idea as to where he was going when he saw in the midst of the sea a rock which looked like white marble. On the top of the rock a little goat was bleating and beckoning to him.

The strangest thing about it all was this : the goat's fleece, instead of being black or white, or a mixture of these two colours like that of other goats, was blue, a bright blue, that reminded him of the hair of that lovely child of long ago.

Oh, how Pinocchio's heart began to beat ! Redoubling his energy, he swam towards the rock. He was already half-way there, when what should he see, rushing towards him on the surface of the water, but a sea monster, with a horrible head, and with its mouth, which was like an abyss, wide open, showing three rows of teeth that would have frightened anyone, even in a picture.

Do you know what this monster was ?

It was no other than that gigantic Shark, which has been mentioned more than once in this history, and which, on account of its dreadful destruction of life and its insatiable voracity, was called " The Attila of the fish and the fishermen."

Poor Pinocchio was terribly frightened at the sight of such a monster. He tried to dodge him, to go some other way, or to swim faster than this terror, but that immense wide-open mouth came right after him, as swift as an arrow.

" Hurry, Pinocchio, for mercy's sake ! " bleated the pretty little goat.

Pinocchio swam desperately, putting forth every ounce of his strength.

" Hasten, Pinocchio, the monster is close behind you ! "

And then Pinocchio swam very much faster than before. " Beware, Pinocchio, the monster is catching up with you ! Here he comes ! Here he comes ! Hurry, for pity's sake, or you will be lost ! "

And Pinocchio swam faster than ever, on, on, on, like a ball out of a gun. He was close to the rock, and the little goat was leaning out over the sea, and holding out her front hoofs to help him out of the water ! . . .

But it was too late ! The monster had reached him, and drawing in his breath he swallowed him as one swallows an egg. He swallowed him so violently and voraciously, and Pinocchio struck so hard against the monster's inside, that he was stunned for a quarter of an hour.

When he came to himself he could not have told where he was. All around him there was a great darkness ; a darkness so thick and profound that he felt as if he had dived head first into a bottle of ink. He listened, but he heard nothing ; only, from time to time, a great blast of wind struck him in the face. At first he did not know where the wind came from, but he soon saw that it came from the monster's lungs. For you should know that the Shark was a great sufferer from asthma, and when he breathed it was like the north wind blowing.

At first Pinocchio tried to pluck up a little courage ; but when he was perfectly sure that he was imprisoned in the Shark's body he began to weep and wail, saying :

" Help ! Help ! Oh, poor me ! Will no one come and save me ? "

" Who could save you, miserable wretch ? " said a voice in the darkness, like a guitar out of tune.

" Who is speaking here ? " asked Pinocchio, turning cold with fear.

" It's me. I'm a poor Tunny, who was swallowed with you. What kind of a fish are you ? "

" I have nothing to do with fishes. I am a marionette."

" If you are not a fish, why did you come here inside this monster ? "

" I didn't *come* here ; he swallowed me. What are we going to do now, in this dark place ? "

" We must resign ourselves, and wait for the Shark to digest us."

" But I don't want to be digested ! " screamed Pinocchio, beginning to cry again.

" Neither do I want to be digested ! " continued the Tunny, " but I am enough of a philosopher to be able to console myself by thinking that when one is a born Tunny, it is more dignified to die under water than under oil."

" Foolishness ! " cried Pinocchio.

" That is my opinion," replied the Tunny, " and opinions, as the Tunny politicians say, should be respected."

" However that may be, I want to get out of this, I want to escape . . ."

" Escape then, if you can ! "

" Is he very big, this Shark that has swallowed us ? "

" His body is more than half a mile long, without counting his tail."

While they were talking in the darkness, it seemed to Pinocchio that he saw a gleam of light, very far off.

" Whatever can that little light be that is so far away ? " asked Pinocchio.

" It's probably one of our companions in distress who, like us, is waiting to be digested."

" I'm going to find him. Mightn't it be some old fish who could tell me how to escape from this place ? "

" I hope it may be, dear marionette."

" Good-bye, Tunny."

" Good-bye, marionette, good luck to you."

"Where shall we meet again ? "

" Who knows ? It's better not to think about it ! "

CHAPTER THIRTY-FIVE

Pinocchio Finds in the Body of the Shark . . . whom does he Find ? Read this Chapter and you will See

As soon as Pinocchio had said good-bye to the Tunny, he began to feel his way in the darkness inside the Shark's body, working his way along, step by step, towards that tiny, flickering light, so far away.

As he walked along, his feet slipped in puddles of fat, greasy water, and there was such a strong smell of fried fish that he felt as if he were in the middle of Lent.

The farther he went the more distinctly he could see that little light. He walked and walked, and at last, when he reached it, what did he find ? I will give you a thousand guesses. He found a little table all set, with a lighted candle stuck in a green glass bottle, and sitting at the table there was an old man, as white as if he were made of snow, or whipped cream. He was eating some live fish, that were so very much alive that sometimes they hopped out of his mouth while he was eating them.

At the sight poor Pinocchio felt such a sudden rush of joy that he came within an inch of fainting away. He wanted to laugh, to cry, to say a hundred things, and instead he only stammered broken words, without any sense. At last he managed to utter a cry of joy, and opening his arms wide, he threw them around the old man's neck, shouting :

" Oh, Daddy ! my Daddy ! Have I found you at last ? I will never leave you again, never, never, never ! "

" So my eyes do not deceive me ? " said the old man, rubbing them vigorously. " Are you really my dear Pinocchio ? "

" Yes, yes, it's really, truly me ! You haven't forgotten me, have you ? Oh, my dear Daddy, how good you are ! And to think that I . . . Oh ! but when you know how many disasters have befallen me, and how many things have gone wrong ?

You know, poor Daddy, that the very day that you sold your coat to buy me a primer so that I could go to school, I ran away to see the marionettes, and the Showman was going to put me in the fire, so his sheep would be well roasted : it was he who gave me five gold pieces to carry home to you, but I met the Fox and the Cat, and they took me to the Red Crab Inn, where they ate like hungry wolves, and I went away alone in the night, and I met assassins who ran after me, and I ran, and they ran after me, and I ran, and they ran right after me, and I ran until they hung me to a branch of the big oak, where the beautiful child with blue hair sent a carriage for me, and the doctors when they saw me said right away, ' If he isn't dead it's a sign that he's alive,' and then I told a lie, and my nose began to grow so I couldn't get out of the room ; and so I went with the Fox and the Cat to bury the four gold pieces, for I spent one at the Inn, and the parrot laughed at me, and instead of two thousand gold pieces I didn't find anything, and when the Judge heard that he put me in prison right away, to please the thieves, and when I got out I saw a bunch of grapes in a field and I was caught in a trap, and the farmer was perfectly right to put a dog collar on me, and make me guard the henhouse, but he found I was innocent and let me go, and the serpent with the tail that smoked began to laugh, and burst a blood vessel, and so I came back to the home of the lovely child, but she was dead, and the Dove saw me crying and said, ' I saw your father building a boat to go and look for you,' and I said, ' Oh, if only I had wings, too ! ' and he said, ' Do you want to go to your father ? ' and I said, ' Do I ? But who will take me ? ' and he said, ' I will take you,' and I said, ' How ? ' and he said ' Get on my back,' and so we flew all night long, and in the morning we saw the fishermen looking out over the sea, and they said, ' There's a poor man in a little boat, who is going to be drowned,' and I knew you at once, for although you were so far away, my heart told me it was you, and I made signs to you to come back . . ."

" I knew you, too," said Geppetto, " and I should have been glad to come back, but how could I ? The waves ran so high and an enormous one upset my boat. A horrible Shark that was nearby swam quickly towards me as soon as he saw me in the water, and sticking out his tongue he lapped me up as if I had been a tart."

"How long have you been shut up in here?" asked Pinocchio.

"It is two years since that day: two years, my Pinocchio, that have seemed like two centuries!"

"How have you managed to live here? And where did you find the candle? And the matches to light it, who gave them to you?"

"I will tell you the whole story. In that same tempest which overturned my boat, a merchant ship was also sunk. The sailors were all saved, but the ship was wrecked. The Shark had an excellent appetite that day, and after he had swallowed me, he swallowed the ship, too."

"What! Did he swallow it in one mouthful?" cried Pinocchio in amazement.

"All in one mouthful, only he spat out the mainmast, because it got between his teeth, like a fish bone. Luckily for me the ship was laden with cans of preserved meat, and biscuits or toasted bread, and bottles of wine, and dried grapes, and cheese, and coffee, and sugar, and candles, and matches. With all these supplies I have been able to live for two years, but now I am at the end of everything. There is nothing more in the pantry, and this candle that you see is the very last one."

"And then?"

"And then, my dear, we shall be left in the dark."

"Then, Daddy," said Pinocchio, "there is no time to be lost. Let us try to find a way to escape immediately."

"To escape . . . but how?"

"We can escape by way of the Shark's mouth; throw ourselves into the sea, and swim for the shore."

"That sounds very fine, dear Pinocchio, but I can't swim."

"That doesn't matter, I am a good swimmer. You can get on my back, and I will carry you safe and sound to the shore."

"It is useless, my boy," replied Geppetto, shaking his head

and smiling sadly. " Do you think it possible that a marionette like you, only three feet tall, would be strong enough to swim with me on his back ? "

" Try me, and you will see ! At any rate, if it is written that we must die, we shall have the consolation of dying in each other's arms."

Without any more words Pinocchio took the candle, and going ahead to show the way he said to his father :

" Follow me, and don't be afraid."

They travelled like this for some time, all through the body and the stomach of the Shark. When they came to his great throat they stopped to look around, and seize the right moment for their flight.

Now the Shark was very old, and since he was a great sufferer from asthma and palpitation of the heart, he had to sleep with his mouth open : so when Pinocchio came to his throat and looked upwards, he could see a broad band of starry sky and a large bright moon.

" This is just the right moment to escape," he whispered, turning to his father. " The Shark is sleeping like a dormouse. The sea is smooth, and it's as light as day. Come, Daddy, follow me, and in a few moments we shall be free."

No sooner said than done. They climbed up the monster's throat, and when they were in that immense mouth they walked along his tongue on the tips of their toes. His tongue was so long and large that it looked like a broad garden path. They were just ready to jump down into the sea when the Shark sneezed, shaking them so violently that they fell back into his stomach.

The candle was extinguished by their fall and father and son were left in the dark.

" Now what shall we do ? " said Pinocchio anxiously.

" Now, my son, we are surely lost ! "

" Why are we lost ? Give me your hand, Daddy, and be careful not to slip."

" Where are you going ? "

" We must try again. Come with me, and don't be afraid."

With these words Pinocchio took his father by the hand, and always walking on tiptoe, they went again up the monster's throat, walked along his tongue, and climbed over the three rows of teeth. Before jumping into the sea the marionette said to his father :

" Now get on my back, and hang on tight. I will do the rest."

As soon as Geppetto was settled on his back, Pinocchio jumped into the water and began to swim. The sea was as smooth as oil ; the moon shone brightly, and the Shark continued to sleep so soundly that he would not have been disturbed by the firing of a cannon.

Chapter Thirty-Six

At last Pinocchio Ceases to be a Marionette and Becomes a Real Boy

WHILE Pinocchio was swimming for the shore as fast as he could, he noticed that his father, who was sitting on his back with his legs in the water, was shivering violently, as if he had the ague.

Was he shivering with cold, or fear? Who knows? Perhaps a little of both. But Pinocchio thought he was afraid, and he said by way of comforting him:

" Courage, Daddy, in a few minutes we shall reach the shore and be safe."

" But where is this blessed shore? " inquired the old man, becoming more uneasy every moment, and squinting like a sailor when he threads a needle. " Here I am looking in every direction. and I see nothing but sea and sky."

" But I see the shore, too," said the marionette. " You know I am like a cat; I can see better at night than in the daytime."

Poor Pinocchio pretended to be cheerful, but he was beginning to feel discouraged. He was growing weaker, and he breathed with difficulty; in short, his strength was almost gone, and the shore was still far away.

He swam until his breath filled him: then he turned to his father and said brokenly:

" Daddy, help me . . . I am dying! "

Father and son were about to drown together, when a voice like a guitar out of tune said:

" Who is it that's dying? "

" It's me and my poor father! "

" I recognise that voice! You are Pinocchio! "

" Precisely: and you? "

" I am the Tunny, your companion in the Shark's body."

" How did you escape ? "

" I followed your example. You showed the way; I followed you, and I, too, escaped."

" Dear Tunny, you have come just in time ! I beg you, for the love you bear your children, the little Tunnies, to help us, or we are lost."

" Willingly ! With all my heart. Take hold of my tail, and let me tow you. You will be on the beach in four minutes."

You may be sure that Geppetto and Pinocchio accepted the invitation instantly; but instead of taking hold of the Tunny's tail, they found it more convenient to sit on his back.

" Are we too heavy ? " asked Pinocchio.

" Heavy ! Why you're light as a feather ! It's as if I had two empty sea shells on my back," replied the Tunny, who was as large and robust as a two-year-old calf.

Arrived at the beach Pinocchio jumped down first, and then helped his father to do the same. Then he turned to the Tunny and said in a trembling voice :

" My friend, you have saved my father's life ! I have no words with which to thank you. Will you permit me to give you a kiss, as a token of my everlasting gratitude ? "

The Tunny put his nose out of the water, and Pinocchio, kneeling on the groud, imprinted an affectionate kiss on his mouth. At this sign of real, spontaneous affection the Tunny, who was not accustomed to anything of the sort, was so moved that, ashamed to be seen crying like a baby, he dived under the water, and disappeared.

Meanwhile the sun had risen.

Pinocchio gave his arm to Geppetto, who was so weak that he could scarcely stand, and said :

" Lean on me, dear Daddy, and let us go. We will walk very slowly, like snails, and when we are tired we will stop and rest."

" And where shall we go ? " inquired Geppetto.

" We will look for a house, or a cabin where we can ask for a bit of bread, and a little straw for a bed."

They had not taken a hundred steps when they saw by the roadside two ugly faces, waiting to beg of the passers-by.

They were the Fox and the Cat, but so changed you would hardly have known them. The Cat had pretended to be blind until he had actually become so ; the Fox had grown old, and his fur was so moth-eaten that it had entirely disappeared on one side, and he had even lost his tail. That's the way it goes. That sorry thief had fallen into such depths of poverty that he had been forced, one day, to sell his beautiful tail to a travelling pedlar who wanted it to drive away the flies.

" Oh, Pinocchio," whined the Fox, " give something to two poor invalids."

" Invalids," repeated the Cat.

" Good-bye, impostors," replied the marionette ; " you fooled me once, but you never will again."

" Believe me, Pinocchio, we are truly poor and unfortunate ! "

" Poor and unfortunate ! " repeated the Cat.

" If you are poor, you deserve to be. Remember the proverb : ' Stolen money bears no fruit ! ' Good-bye, impostors ! "

" Have pity on us ! "

" On us ! "

" Good-bye impostors, remember the proverb : ' The devil's flour is all bran.' "

" Do not abandon us ! "

" Us ! " repeated the Cat.

" Good-bye, impostors ! Remember the proverb : ' He who steals his neighbour's cloak, usually dies without a shirt.' "

So saying, Pinocchio and Geppetto went peacefully on their way, but they had gone only another hundred steps when they saw at the end of a little path in a meadow a pretty little cottage made of straw, with a roof of bricks and tiles.

" Someone must live in that cottage," said Pinocchio. " Let us rap on the door."

" Who is it ? " said a tiny voice inside.

" A poor father and his poor son, without bread and without a home," replied the marionette.

" Turn the key and the door will open," said the little voice.

Pinocchio turned the key and the door flew open. They went in and looked all around, but they saw no one.

" Where can the man of the house be ? " said Pinocchio in astonishment.

" Here I am, up here."

Father and son looked up at the ceiling, and there on a little cross-beam was the Talking Cricket.

" Oh, my dear Cricket," said Pinocchio, with a polite bow.

" So I am your ' dear Cricket ' now, am I ? Do you remember when you drove me from your house by throwing a mallet at me ? "

" You are right, Cricket ; drive me away, too, throw a mallet at me, too, but have pity on my poor father."

" I will have pity on father and son ; but I wanted to remind you of the cruel treatment I received, in order to teach you that in this world we should treat everyone kindly when it is possible, so that we may be treated kindly in the day of our need."

" You are right, Cricket, you are perfectly right, and I will remember your lesson. But tell me, how did you manage to buy this pretty cottage ? "

" This cottage was given to me yesterday, by a fine goat with beautiful blue hair."

" What has become of the goat ? "

" I don't know."

" When will she return ? "

" She will never return. She went away yesterday, very sad, and bleating as if to say : ' Poor Pinocchio, now I shall never see him again ! The Shark must have devoured him by this time ! ' "

" Did she say that ? It must have been the Fairy, it was surely the Fairy, my dear little Fairy ! " shouted Pinocchio, sobbing bitterly and shedding floods of tears.

When he had had a good cry, he wiped his eyes and made

up a comfortable bed of straw for old Geppetto. Then he said to the Talking Cricket :

" Tell me, Cricket, where can I get a cup of milk for my poor father ? "

" Giangio, the gardener, lives three fields from here. He keeps cows. If you go there you can get some milk."

Pinocchio ran all the way to Giangio's house ; but the gardener said :

" How much milk do you want ? "

" I want a cupful."

" A cup of milk costs a penny. First give me the penny."

" I haven't even a farthing," replied Pinocchio, very sadly and shame-facedly.

" That's too bad," replied the gardener. " If you haven't even a farthing, neither have I a drop of milk."

" Patience ! " said Pinocchio, and he turned to go away.

" Wait a minute," said Giangio, " perhaps we can make a bargain. Will you turn the windlass for me ? "

" What is the windlass ? "

" It's that machine that brings up water from the cistern to water the orchard."

" I will try."

" Well, if you will draw a hundred buckets of water, I will give you a cup of milk."

" All right."

Giangio took the marionette into the orchard and showed him how to turn the windlass. Pinocchio set to work at once, but before he had drawn the hundred buckets of water he was dripping with sweat from head to foot. He had never worked like that before.

" My donkey has done this work until now," said the gardener, " but the poor beast is dying to-day."

" May I go and see him ? " asked Pinocchio.

" Certainly."

When Pinocchio entered the stable, he saw a fine donkey lying on the straw. He was dying of hunger and hard work. He looked closely at him and said to himself in great agitation :

" I believe I know that donkey ; his features are not new to me." And bending over him he said in donkey dialect :

" Who are you ? "

At this question the dying donkey opened his eyes and stammered in the same dialect :

" I . . . am . . . Lamp . . . wick . . ." after which he closed his eyes and expired.

" Oh, poor Lampwick ! " murmured Pinocchio, and taking a handful of straw he wiped away a tear that was running down his cheek.

" Are you so sorry for a donkey that doesn't cost you anything ? " said the gardener. " What shall I do, who bought him for cash down ? "

" I'll tell you . . . he was my friend."

" Your friend ? "

" A schoolmate of mine."

" What ! " shouted Giangio, bursting out laughing. " What ! you had a donkey for a schoolmate ! Fine lessons you must have learned ! "

The marionette was so shamed by these words that he made no reply, but took his cup of milk and went back to the cottage.

From that day onward, for more than five months, he rose before daybreak every morning and turned the windlass, in order to earn the cup of milk that was so good for his father. And not content with this, he learned in his spare time to weave panniers and baskets of reeds. These he sold for enough to pay all their expenses. Among other things he made a fine little cart in which to take his father out for a ride and a breath of fresh air when the weather was good.

Every evening he practised reading and writing. For a few pennies he had purchased a large book in the town nearby. The index and frontispiece were missing, but it served its purpose very well. He whittled a pen out of a little twig, and having neither ink nor inkwell, he used a little bottle of cherry and blackberry juice.

In fact, by reason of his ingenuity and his willingness to

work, his father, whose health was still very poor, was able to live quite comfortably. He was even able to save two shillings to buy himself a new suit.

One morning he said to his father:

" I'm going to market to-day, to buy myself a new jacket and a cap and a pair of shoes. When I return," he added, laughing, " I shall be so fine that you will mistake me for a grand gentleman."

He felt perfectly happy and contented as he ran along. Suddenly he heard someone calling him; he turned and saw a fine snail crawling out of the hedge.

" Don't you recognise me ? " said the Snail.

" Perhaps, but I'm not sure . . ."

" Don't you remember that Snail who was the blue-haired Fairy's chambermaid ? Don't you remember that time I came downstairs to let you in, and found you with your foot sticking in the door ? "

" I remember everything ! " cried Pinocchio. " Tell me quickly, kind Snail, where did you leave my good Fairy ? What is she doing ? Has she forgiven me ? Does she still remember me ? Does she love me still ? Is she very far from here ? Can I go and find her ? "

Pinocchio asked all these questions as fast as he could, without stopping to breathe; but the Snail replied with her usual deliberation :

" My dear Pinocchio, the poor Fairy lies in bed in a hospital ! "

" In a hospital ! "

" It's only too true. Overcome by a thousand disasters, she is very, very ill, and she has no money with which to buy even a crust of bread."

" Is it possible ? Oh, what dreadful news ! Oh, the poor Fairy ! the poor Fairy ! If I had a million pounds, I would run and give them to her ; but I have only two shillings . . . here they are ; I was just going to buy myself a new suit. Take them, Snail, and carry them quickly to the kind Fairy."

" But your new suit ? "

" What do I care for a new suit! I would even sell these rags I wear if it would help her. Go, Snail, hurry. If you will come back in two days, I can give you a little more. I have worked until now to maintain my father; henceforth I will work five hours longer every day to maintain my kind mother, also. Good-bye, Snail, I will expect you in two days."

The Snail, contrary to her custom, began to run like a lizard in summer.

When Pinocchio returned his father inquired:

" Where is your new suit? "

" I couldn't find one that fitted me. Patience! I will buy it another time."

That evening, instead of working until ten o'clock, Pinocchio worked until the clock struck twelve; and instead of making eight baskets, he made sixteen.

Then he went to bed and fell asleep. As he slept he dreamed that he saw the Fairy, lovely and smiling, who gave him a kiss, saying:

" Bravo, Pinocchio! In return for your generosity, I forgive you all your past escapades. Children who love their parents, and help them when they are sick and poor, are worthy of praise and affection, even if they cannot be called models of obedience and good conduct. Be wise in the future, and you will be happy."

Then the dream ended, and Pinocchio awoke, full of wonder.

You can easily imagine how astonished he was when he saw that he was no longer a marionette, but a real boy like other boys. He looked around, but instead of the straw walls of the cottage, he saw a pretty little room simply but beautifully furnished and decorated. He jumped out of bed, and found a lovely new suit, a new cap, and a pair of boots as pretty as a picture.

As soon as he was dressed, he naturally put his hands in his pockets, and what did he find there but a little ivory purse on which these words were written:

" The blue-haired Fairy returns Pinocchio's two shillings, and thanks him for his generosity." He opened the purse, and instead of two silver shillings, there were twenty gold pieces, fresh from the mint.

Then he went to look in the mirror, but he did not recognise himself. He no longer saw the usual image of a wooden marionette, but the expressive, intelligent features of a fine boy, with brown hair and blue eyes, who looked as happy and joyful as an Easter Sunday.

In the midst of all these wonders coming one after the other, Pinocchio no longer knew whether he was really awake or asleep with his eyes open.

" And my father, where is he ? " he cried suddenly. He went into the next room where he saw old Geppetto, well, and lively, and good-natured, just as he was before. He had taken up again his old art of wood-carving, and at that moment he was designing a beautiful cornice, richly ornamented with leaves and flowers, and heads of animals.

" Daddy, explain this to me : what is the meaning of this sudden change ? " asked Pinocchio, throwing his arms around his neck and kissing him.

" This sudden change in our circumstances is all owing to you," replied Geppetto.

" Why is it owing to me ? "

" Because when children who were naughty become good, it gives a new and smiling appearance to the whole family."

" And the old wooden Pinocchio, where is he ? "

" There he is," replied Geppetto, pointing to a large marionette that was leaning against a chair with his head on one side, his arms dangling, and his legs doubled up and crossed, so that it was a miracle that he stood there at all.

Pinocchio turned and looked at him for a little while, and then he said to himself contentedly :

" How ridiculous I was when I was a marionette ! And how glad I am that I have become a real boy ! "

THE END